You Can Hurry Love

# You Can Hurry Love

SHERRY KYLE

*"Forget the former things; do not dwell on the past. See, I am doing a new thing! Now it springs up; do you not perceive it? I am making a way in the wilderness and streams in the wasteland."*

*~ Isaiah 43:18-19*

# CHAPTER ONE

Megan Conway opened the mauve-colored envelope. She lifted the flap of the second envelope, and pulled out a single piece of stationery, her eyes focusing on the words of the wedding invitation.

Stephanie Marie Whitcomb
and
Chase Thomas Donovan
request the honor of your presence
at their marriage

Megan's mouth went dry and her hands shook as she slunk down on her bed. Her ex-boyfriend of six years was getting married? *This Saturday?* After *their* break-up four months ago?

She stood and paced the room, her gut twisting into a knot—not because she wasn't marrying the debonair lawyer. After all, *she* was the one who broke off their engagement. She just couldn't bear the thought that Chase had found someone so quickly. It took a long time for two people to fall in love and make such a big commitment. Didn't it?

Her heart rate accelerated as her eyes drifted back to the paper still clutched in her hand. Why would he send her an invitation? And so close to the event? Did he think it would help her move on? Or did he want to rub it in her face? Well, she wouldn't go. Couldn't.

Megan ran to the bathroom, feeling as though she might be sick. She leaned against the bathroom counter and inhaled several slow deep breaths before splashing cold water on her face. She tamped her cheeks dry with a hand towel and stared at herself in the mirror.

Two weeks ago she'd sent off her twenty kindergarteners for the summer, cleaned her small apartment, painted her bathroom, and hung new curtains—a great achievement for someone tired after a year of teaching. But now after receiving the wedding invitation, she found herself ready to get back to work—to busy herself so she wouldn't think about the years wasted on Chase Donovan.

Her brows cinched. She hadn't even taken a summer vacation.

Megan returned to her bedroom and tossed the invitation on her dresser, a new plan quickly forming. She pulled open her top drawer and dug under her mound of clean socks for the brochure she'd hidden there. The Monterey Plaza Hotel and Spa was her ultimate dream vacation, the perfect honeymoon she'd hoped to plan with Chase. But it wasn't until he passed the bar exam that he'd shown his true colors. She couldn't be the trophy wife he wanted. He didn't understand teaching was her passion and she'd continue whether married or not.

She stared at the picture of the dramatic hotel perched over the Monterey Bay, the ideal place to enjoy the gentle sounds of the surf and the scent of the sea air. A quick drive from Sacramento and she'd be there—a perfect spa getaway to keep her mind off Chase and his new bride.

Before she changed her mind, Megan punched in her sister's phone number. Heather answered on the third ring. The words tumbled out in quick succession—from Chase's new love to a trip down the coast.

"So you received the wedding invitation, huh?" Her sister's tone indicated she'd anticipated this conversation.

"You knew about this? Why didn't you tell me?"

"I just got the invitation yesterday. I'm really sorry, Meg."

"Please come with me to Monterey," Megan said. "The way you work nonstop, I'm sure you need the break. Just think of it—massages, facials. The place is known for its spa treatments."

"Not everyone has time off in the summer." Heather's tone softened. "Maybe it'd be better to just go to the wedding—get some closure. Are you sure you want to run from your problems?"

"Who's running?" Megan squeezed her eyes shut at the pinched sound of her voice. Even she wasn't convinced. She'd chicken out and stay at home if her sister didn't go with her—but she *needed* to have plans for Saturday.

Better change her tactic.

"When's the last time you did something for yourself?"

"It's been a while. I can't remember the last time I had peace and quiet." Heather sighed. "Honestly, this working from home isn't working out. It's only been a couple of weeks since school ended for the summer, and the kids are driving me crazy."

"Please come with me? It'll do you good."

Megan waited in silence. She could almost hear her sister contemplating the idea.

"Anthony is away on business … let me call my mother-in-law to see if she can watch the kids," Heather finally said.

"Perfect. In the meantime, I'll call the hotel and book a reservation." Megan's voice rose, her excitement growing. "Five whole days of pampering and relaxation. You're going to love it."

"Meg, if it means anything to you, I said we couldn't make the wedding. Family friend or not, no man who breaks my little sister's heart is worth the time of day."

She appreciated her sister's overprotective instincts. "You're forgetting I'm the one who broke up with *him*." It felt good to say it out loud.

"Even so. The wound must still be fresh. It hasn't been that long—"

*Four months, one week, and three days to be exact, but who's counting?*

"Enough about Chase Donovan." And his crazy whirlwind romance. "Let's go on a vacation. You and me— sisters. We'll have the time of our lives." Megan flopped back on her bed, attempting to fill her thoughts with positive things like sun, surf, and all things spa related.

"I'm not made of money. Did I tell you we had to buy a new water heater last week? And the bills are piling up— orthodontist visits, piano lessons, soccer—"

"Did I mention all expenses are paid?" Megan winced at her desperation. Now there was no reason for her sister to change her mind.

"Are you serious? How?" Heather's tone lifted. "Did you win a trip or something? And are you sure you can get reservations on this short of notice?"

"Don't worry about it. I want you to be my guest." Her sister's company was worth depleting her savings account.

And if all the rooms were booked at the Monterey Plaza Hotel and Spa, she'd find an occupancy elsewhere. There was no way she was going to be in town during Chase's wedding.

"We've lived in Sacramento our whole lives and have never stayed in Monterey." Heather's tone sounded wistful.

"You know you want to come—"

"Give me an hour to make arrangements."

"That's the spirit I was looking for." Megan smiled.

After she hung up the phone, she tossed her clothes and bathing suit into her bag. This trip should be her honeymoon, not an escape. Her shoulders sagged, and she blinked back tears. She was the one who had encouraged Chase to go to law school and had stuck by him throughout the years to achieve his dream. Now, *what's-her-name*, Stephanie, was going to reap the rewards of having a lawyer for a husband without living through all the hard work. Megan's head started to throb. Yes, she had to get out of town—the sooner the better.

She picked up the hotel brochure, scanned it for the phone number, and punched in the number.

It might not be her honeymoon, but she planned on having the time of her life.

Lucas Hunter tossed shorts and T-shirts into his duffel bag, preparing himself for the ribbing from his extended family.

His grandma Ruby had told him more than once that she wanted to see him get married and become a father before she entered heaven. Did he dare show up for the family reunion without a woman by his side? He'd hate to disappoint her again, but he was about to do just that. It couldn't be helped. He hadn't found the right woman—yet.

Besides, thirty wasn't too old. Some of his best friends, including Daniel, had only recently tied the knot. If it weren't for Kimberly's love for Daniel's German Shepherd, they might not have met and gotten married. As a veterinarian Lucas loved animals, but he'd never go so far as posting on an online dating site like Daniel and Kimberly had done. After all, how hard was it to find a woman who put faith, family, and friends above everything else?

Lucas scooped up his toiletries from the bathroom counter and dropped them into his bag. Grandma Ruby wasn't getting any younger. He'd noticed a slight hunch to her shoulders and a shuffle in her steps the last time the family got together. And according to his mom, cancer could shorten his grandma's life dramatically if the biopsy came back positive. The weeklong vacation at a fancy hotel in Monterey to celebrate his grandma's eightieth birthday was on her bucket list—and her dime. She'd insisted.

A knock sounded on the front door and Lucas opened it.

"Ready to go?" Daniel asked.

"You sure don't mind taking care of Goldie?" Lucas went down on one knee and scratched behind his golden retriever's left ear.

"Na. She gets along great with Bruno. The two of them play like pups." Daniel patted the dog's head. "Don't you, girl?"

"I hate to leave her." Lucas wrapped an arm around the dog's neck. "I usually take her with me. Camping is more my style." He covered the dog's ears. "She's going to think

I abandoned her. And you know what she does when that happens. She eats everything in sight."

"Don't worry, man. She'll be fine. Between Kimberly and me, we've got you covered. You have nothing to worry about."

"Call me if you need anything, and make sure you leave a message. You know Grandma Ruby, she's got a ton of family things planned—"

"In that case, have a nice trip and I'll see you when you get back." Daniel took the leash from Lucas's hand and hooked it on the dog's collar.

He handed Daniel a bag of dog food, her bowl, and favorite blanket.

"So what are you going to do about the woman situation?" Daniel attempted to hide a grin as he gathered the dog's supplies.

"Not you, too!" He jabbed his friend in the shoulder.

Daniel held up a hand. "Just kidding. Lighten up." Goldie tugged on the leash, jostling Daniel's arm further. "I know how your grandma's been bugging you lately. I'm just saying—"

"Thanks for watching Goldie for me. I'll be by to pick her up as soon as I get back."

"Have a good time. Too bad Kimberly doesn't have a friend who could join you. Someone to stop the whispers behind your back." Daniel tossed his words over his shoulder as he and Goldie made their way to Daniel's truck.

Lucas shut the door and pushed down the frustration.

Why couldn't his friend leave him alone? It wasn't like he wasn't interested or looking. He always believed God's timing was perfect. He just had to wait until she was placed into his life.

He zipped up his duffel bag and turned off the lights. Once in the garage, he flung his bag into the back of his SUV.

*Here goes nothing.*

# CHAPTER TWO

Megan stood with her feet frozen to the floor and her mouth agape inside the lobby of the Monterey Plaza Hotel and Spa. It was everything she'd hoped for. The mahogany-colored woodwork and the view of the ocean through the large windows caused her breath to hitch.

Heather came up beside her, pulling on the handle of her rolling suitcase. A computer bag hung on her shoulder. "It's beautiful, simply elegant."

"I knew it would be." Megan smiled. "I'll check us in at the front desk."

"I'll wait right here." Heather pulled out her phone from her purse. "I need to check on a few e-mails."

Megan nodded and moved forward. They were fortunate someone had cancelled at the last minute. She glanced at her watch. 4 p.m. Their room should be ready.

Her bag bumped into someone on the way to the counter. Megan glanced over her shoulder. A handsome man with dark hair and broad shoulders turned toward her.

"Oh, pardon me." She smiled apologetically then continued on to the front desk.

"May I help you?" the female clerk asked.

"Yes, I'd like to check in. The name's Megan Conway." She fiddled with the hem of her cotton blouse, something her sister told her she did when she was nervous or excited. Today, she was both.

The woman scanned the computer screen for her reservation. "There you are. You're staying in one of our deluxe ocean view rooms with a balcony. Would you like one key or two?"

"Two, please." She couldn't help but notice the woman's creamy complexion. Megan's cheeks tingled at the thought of the facial she and Heather hoped to schedule.

"Here you are. I'm also including a map of our amenities." The woman's manicured nails matched the picture-perfect smile she passed Megan's way. Would she feel as relaxed and put together by the time she left the hotel?

"Thank you." Megan clasped the keys and turned around to find her sister ending a phone call.

Lines etched Heather's forehead, and she worked her lower lip. "That was my boss. He expects the bookkeeping to be done by the end of the week. Good thing I brought work with me. Five days of silence is what I need, but I'm afraid it won't be the vacation you expected—"

Megan stopped her with a hand. Suddenly she was glad she'd packed a few novels. It looked like she'd be spending a lot of time on the beach—alone. "You'll need to take breaks. We can still do all the things we talked about on the way here, right?" Her voice rose, anticipating Heather's response.

"I hope so, but I can't promise. Mr. Carmichael e-mailed me a list of accounts as long as my arm. I'm sorry, but work comes first."

Megan held up a key. "The sooner you get started, the quicker we'll have time to play."

"Thanks. You're the best." Heather snatched the key out of Megan's hand and hurried to the elevator.

What had just happened? The trip had barely begun and she felt as though it had just ended.

Lucas didn't mean to eavesdrop, but the striking woman who'd bumped into him earlier drew him like water to sand. It appeared the woman's friend had work to do.

He recalled Daniel's words. *"Too bad Kimberly doesn't have a friend who could join you. Someone to stop the whispers behind your back."*

Grandma Ruby might not be around for much longer. The best birthday present he could give her would be to have a woman by his side.

An idea formed. Did he dare offer to pay the blonde-haired woman's hotel bill if she pretended to be his girlfriend for the week? That would stop his family from bugging him. Plus, it would please his grandmother. But would the woman go for the idea? Seemed like a preposterous thing to do, but under the circumstances . . .

She moved toward the elevator, dragging her luggage behind her.

It was now or never.

Before she disappeared.

Lucas strode toward her. "Excuse me," he called.

The woman turned around.

"This may sound crazy—"

"Oh, you're the one I almost flattened in the lobby. No lasting damage, I hope." A smile tugged at her lips.

"What? Yes. Oh, no big deal, really." He fumbled over his words. He stopped himself, then continued. "But I *would* like to talk to you about something else. I have a plan that might work for both of us."

Her eyes widened, but no words came.

How could he help her understand? "You see, my family is having a reunion at the hotel for my Grandma Ruby's eightieth birthday, everyone except my uncle Joe. He cancelled this morning." Better not go down that rabbit trail. Truthfully, it didn't surprise him. Uncle Joe hadn't joined the family in quite some time. Everyone had a black sheep in the family, and Uncle Joe was definitely it. Lucas pushed that thought to the back of his mind, and focused on the woman in front of him and the reason behind their conversation. "My grandmother has the whole week planned with fun activities—"

"And you're telling me this because?" She bit her lip and wrinkled her brow. Even perplexed, this woman had an endearing quality about her.

"I'd like to ask you to be my date—for the next five days." Why'd he have to go and blurt it out like that? He expected nothing less than a slap on the face for his boldness.

She took a step back. "Your what?"

"Let me start over. According to my grandmother, I should've been married years ago. I know this sounds insane, but if you could meet my grandmother you'd be doing me a huge favor."

"I don't even know you."

The woman had a point.

His words were coming out all wrong. *God, help me out here.* "I couldn't help but overhear your friend say she was going to be busy with work—"

"You were spying on me?" Her lips formed a long O, before she pressed them together in a grim line.

"Not spying, per se, just listening in." Lucas shrugged, knowing his reason sounded inadequate. "Ask me anything you want to know. I'm an open book."

"Let me get this straight." She held up a hand. "After I bumped into you, you followed me, eavesdropped on my conversation with my sister, and now you want to bring me to meet your grandmother and pretend we're an item?"

When she put it that way, it sounded like he was stalking her, or a little off his rocker. Or both. "Yes."

She placed the other hand on her hip. "Give me three good reasons why should I trust you?"

What could he say to make her go along with his plan? "I'm from Sacramento."

One perfectly arched eyebrow went up in surprise.

"I work at South Sacramento Pet Hospital," he continued, "and volunteer every week at my church. And I own a golden retriever who loves to watch tennis on television and take long soaks in the tub. Would you like to see some references?" He joked.

"I work at the elementary school around the corner, so I'd say being from Sacramento is reference enough." She folded her arms across her chest. "So what's in it for me?"

Now he had her attention.

"An all-expense paid vacation. I'll pay your hotel bill and whatever else you'd like to do. I hear the hotel gives top-notch spa treatments."

"You'll pay for everything?" By the woman's more relaxed stance, she was considering the idea.

"Plus, you can join my family whenever you wish. We're going to take a surrey bike ride, have s'mores around a campfire, swim, all the things you'd do with your sister if she were available. And don't worry, we won't be alone."

"So all I need to do is pretend I'm your doting girlfriend, and I can have the vacation of my dreams?" Was she actually warming up to the idea?

"You've got it."

She hesitated.

"Please?" He'd also offer her a home-cooked dinner in Sacramento if he knew it would make a difference. But that might send her running—or call for security.

"Okay, I'll do it." Her words came out in a rush.

"Yeah?" The heaviness in Lucas's chest started to lighten.

"Don't ask again or I may change my mind." A smug grin tugged at her lips.

He had to admit, the girl had courage. Attractive too. "I'm Lucas, by the way. Lucas Hunter." He held out his hand.

She slipped her hand in his and shook it firmly. "Megan Conway."

He couldn't imagine being so willing to go along with his crazy plan. There must be something going on behind those mesmerizing hazel eyes to make her so spontaneous.

"After you drop off your luggage, I'd like to meet on the back veranda. We'll have to get our stories straight before I introduce you to my family."

Why did he have the sudden feeling that he was pushing God aside and taking control?

# CHAPTER THREE

Megan rode the elevator to the second floor, her heart in her throat. What had she done? Yes, Lucas Hunter was a nice-looking man, but to pose as his girlfriend? She'd never agreed to do such a crazy thing in all her life. What if he was mentally unstable? Or had inappropriate things on his mind?

The doors opened and she walked out, questioning her decision to accept Lucas's scheme with every step. She meandered down the hall corridor in search of her hotel room. He did say they'd never be alone. That brought her some comfort. Plus, she'd be able to do the activities she had planned and it wouldn't deplete her savings. Besides, it was only for five days. It wasn't as though she was getting married—like her ex-boyfriend!

She hesitated when she reached her hotel door. What would she tell her sister? Heather already assumed she missed Chase. If Megan informed her she was going to pretend to be a stranger's girlfriend, it would only make the situation worse. Her sister would think she'd lost her mind for sure.

Maybe she had.

Inside the room, Heather sat in the middle of one of the queen-sized beds with her laptop open and paperwork spread all around. Her fingers typed furiously, and her lips pressed together in concentration.

Megan grabbed the opportunity to take in the tastefully decorated room. The striped wallpaper and cream duvet contrasted nicely with the pumpkin-colored pillows and the dark wood desk and headboard. An oil painting of a landscape graced one wall. She swung her luggage onto the rack and unzipped it. Maybe she wouldn't have to say anything to her sister—yet. "Don't mind me. I'll unpack quietly."

After putting her clothes in the drawers and running a brush through her hair, she slunk from the room in flip-flops, key in hand and her purse over her shoulder.

Until she got to know Lucas, she'd keep his offer to herself.

"Grandma!" Lucas found Grandma Ruby sitting on the veranda wearing a sunhat and sipping a glass of lemonade. He planted a kiss on her cheek. "I didn't know you'd be here already." His voice faltered. His plan to get acquainted with Megan first before introducing her to the family had backfired.

"I was hoping to see you before everyone came."

Lucas put on his sunglasses. "How'd you know I'd be here?" A sickening feeling filled his gut. Had she overheard him talk with Megan in the lobby?

"I had a feeling." Grandma grinned. "Besides, I called Daniel and heard he'd already picked up Goldie. I've been waiting a good half hour. Isn't the view gorgeous?" She lifted a hand toward the ocean.

He'd have to think fast before Megan arrived. If she did.

"Grandma, are you sure you should be in the sun? Maybe you'd like to go inside. Here, hold onto my arm." Lucas bent slightly and held out his elbow.

"Goodness, no. I'm fine." She batted his arm away. "Come have a seat by your old grandma and tell her what's been going on in your life." It was so typical for her to speak of herself in the third person.

"Waiter?" Grandma waved at the nearest hotel worker. "Would you please bring my grandson a glass of lemonade? And a bowlful of those delicious chocolate-covered strawberries." She passed him a smile.

Lucas glanced at his watch then over his shoulder. Megan was late.

"Am I keeping you from something?" Grandma noticed everything.

"Not at all. I'm right where I'm supposed to be." Lucas ran his sweaty palms down the sides of his shorts. A pang in his chest told him that he should be honest and tell his grandmother that he was still single.

"How's the doctoring going? Busy healing animals?" Grandma Ruby took another sip of her lemonade.

Lucas nodded. "Saved a kitten's life the other day—"

"Sorry I'm late. I almost didn't come." Megan approached with a tentative smile, then stopped short when she noticed the elderly woman by his side.

"Who do we have here?" Grandma Ruby asked.

Lucas nearly choked at the hopeful look on his grandmother's face.

"Hi. You must be Grandma Ruby. I'm Megan Conway." She took his grandmother's hand and squeezed. "Happy Birthday."

"Thank you." Grandma beamed. "Lucas, what a nice surprise. You didn't tell me you'd be bringing a girl to the reunion."

"I didn't know I was coming to the hotel until this morning," Megan said. "It was kind of spur of the moment."

Lucas stood and pulled out a seat for Megan to join them.

"Thank you." She tossed him a wide-eyed look as she sat down.

"You're just in time for some chocolate-covered strawberries," Grandma said. The waiter approached with a small bowlful and a glass of lemonade.

"I love chocolate, but I'm allergic to strawberries." Megan pressed her hands in her lap.

"Oh no, dear. I'm sorry to hear that." Grandma's face puckered. "Lucas, make sure you tell me next time. I would've ordered something else."

There were other things he hadn't told his grandmother—like the fact that the woman sitting beside them was a total stranger. He pushed the glass of lemonade Megan's way and made a mental note of her allergy. *No strawberries.* Lucas snatched one and popped it into his mouth.

"So tell me, how did you two meet?" Grandma Ruby sat forward in her chair.

He had feared the question since he concocted the charade an hour ago. He pointed to his mouth and chewed. He needed a few moments to think of an answer.

"He felt sorry for me." Megan shot him a coy smile.

"Sorry for you? Whatever for? You're a beautiful girl." Grandma adjusted her hat to block the sun.

Megan crossed her legs, and then uncrossed them. Apparently she was as uncomfortable as he. "Lucas had just discovered some news and wanted to make sure I was taken care of."

*Very funny.*

He'd eavesdropped on the sisters' conversation and rescued her from a boring vacation. Nothing more.

"That's our Lucas. He takes care of strays wherever he goes."

Lucas shifted in his seat. "She's hardly a stray, Grandma."

"Oh my." Grandma Ruby chuckled. "That didn't come out right."

If he and Megan couldn't speak in private about their lives, they'd have to give each other clues. "My job as a veterinarian is much different than dating someone." Oh, boy. Had he actually said the 'D' word?

"So the two of you are dating? Glory be!" Grandma clapped her hands together.

"We met a short time ago and are still getting to know each other." Lucas wanted to put out this fire as quickly as possible.

"But you're far enough along to ask her to meet the family. I'd say this is a big step for you, Lucas." Grandma Ruby stood and kissed the top of his head. "It won't be long until the rest of the family arrives. I'm going to scoot and leave you two lovebirds alone. It's time for my afternoon nap."

Grandma Ruby grabbed her cane hooked on the side of the table and hobbled away. "Lucas is finally dating someone," she exclaimed to no one in particular on her way into the hotel.

Lucas's shoulders drooped. *Lovebirds?* He was in a real fix now.

# CHAPTER FOUR

"**R**eady?"

How could one simple word hold so much meaning? Megan attempted to swallow, her mouth dry.

Earlier when Grandma Ruby went to take a nap, Lucas briefed her about his family. Who was who, and how they interacted. Sounded like an interesting bunch.

After breaking up with Chase, she'd vowed not to meet another man's family until she was close to having a diamond ring on her finger. It hurt too badly. She missed Chase's younger sister's fun personality and his mother's homemade cooking. Mostly, she missed spending time at the Donovan house after church on Sundays. They'd watch football, eat pizza, and joke about how intense Chase and his father were when rooting for the San Francisco 49ers. Did Stephanie, Chase's fiancée, now take her place on the sectional sofa? The thought jarred her.

Megan ran her hand down the sides of her floral skirt and played with the hem of her cardigan sweater, just the right attire for a balmy Monterey evening.

"What's the matter?" Lucas asked. "You're as white as a ghost."

"It's nothing." She shrugged. "I guess I never imagined myself in this type of situation."

Lucas shot her a wry grin. "That makes two of us."

He led her into Schooners, the hotel's stunning seafood restaurant, for a family dinner. They wound their way through the candlelit tables to the outdoor patio suspended over the waters of the Monterey Bay.

Megan's throat constricted. In her heart she knew she was over Chase, but the thought made her palms sweat. On the drive to Monterey, she'd imagined what it would have been like to go to this restaurant with Chase, not a dark-haired veterinarian who was a stranger, no less.

But she had to admit, Lucas made a handsome image in his polo shirt and khaki cargo pants. They fit his frame nicely. She wasn't embarrassed to have a meal with him, as shallow as that sounded. And he must have been attracted to her in some way, or he wouldn't have asked her to pose as his girlfriend in the first place.

"Here they are." Grandma Ruby clapped her hands and gestured toward the two empty seats. A few small square tables were pushed together to form one large rectangular one. A heater lamp was situated next to Grandma Ruby despite the fact it was seventy degrees.

Lucas held out Megan's chair and waited for her to get comfortable before taking the seat beside her. He had already proven he was a gentleman, but were his manners for her or his family's benefit?

Megan found a dozen pairs of eyes staring at her as she placed her napkin on her lap. She smiled nervously and bit her lower lip to keep it from trembling.

"Everyone, this is Megan." Lucas placed his hand on the back of her chair. "She's going to be hanging out with us this week. Please be nice to her and don't ask her a million questions."

Lucas's family laughed good-naturedly and a chorus of *nice-to-meet-yous* went around the table.

"Of course we'll be kind," Grandma Ruby said. "We're just not used to seeing you with a girl is all. It's been, what? Three years?"

*Three years?* Megan didn't know whether she should be flattered or concerned.

"Grandma!" Lucas's complexion deepened. He stood. "Maybe this was a bad idea."

A salt-and-pepper version of Lucas motioned him back into his chair. "Sit down, Son. You don't want to miss out. Schooners is known for their seafood." His dad looked like a kind man.

"Don't mind Grandma," the young man, presumably Lucas's brother, Jacob, whispered into Megan's ear. "Lucas is the oldest grandson and she's been wanting him to date for a few years now. Me? I've got it made. Until Lucas ties the knot, she leaves me and my love life alone."

If Megan weren't so self-conscious, she would've laughed out loud. Instead, she pressed her lips together, stifling a giggle. It appeared Jacob knew exactly where he stood. As the younger sibling, Megan could relate. Her parents pushed her sister Heather into wanting marriage and babies and had never made a big issue with her. Maybe if they had, she would've dumped Chase years ago. A satisfying thought, even though she never could've done it. It wasn't until he had the official title of "lawyer" that he'd changed.

"So, what looks good to you, Lucas?" The beautiful middle-aged woman sitting beside his father held up a menu, focusing the attention on the reason for their gathering. His mother, Megan presumed, smiled with lips a nice shade of red, and her eyes beckoned everyone to peruse the selections.

Megan opened her menu, glancing over the top at the rest of Lucas's family. The young woman sitting beside Lucas started chattering about her recent high school graduation and college plans. Must be his sister, Kaitlyn. Megan couldn't see the girl's face, but her hands moved this way and that, obviously excited about what the next year would bring.

On the far end of the table sat a couple lost in their own conversation. Lucas had shared about his aunt Mary and how she'd eloped with Robert when she was only eighteen. Even though the marriage was strong and had lasted, Robert's lack of faith had been a bone of contention with Grandma Ruby. Mary playfully bumped Robert's shoulder and gave him a coy smile. The pair still had eyes for each other.

Lucas leaned close. "What would you like to eat?"

Megan caught a whiff of his musky cologne, his nearness doing a number on her senses. *Focus, Megan, focus!* "I was considering the Burrata salad." The creamy mozzarella, tomatoes, balsamic syrup, and shaved Fiscalini cheese enticed her.

"Will that be enough?" He leaned closer. "You're not one of those girls who barely eats, are you?"

"I assure you, I eat plenty." Megan lifted her menu to cover her mouth. "I went exploring after we met and grabbed a bowl of clam chowder."

"Weren't sure you'd come, huh?"

Megan smiled. "A girl has to be prepared—"

"What are you two whispering about?" Kaitlyn interrupted.

Lucas set down his menu. "How girls never like to eat—"

"Kaitlyn, want to share an appetizer? How about the Caprese pizza?" Megan shot his sister a grin.

"Sure," Kaitlyn said. "I like the way you think."

Lucas folded his arms across his chest. "The two of you will have to give me a slice since I'm sitting between you."

"You could always trade seats with me. I'd love to get to know your girlfriend." Kaitlyn looked hopeful.

Megan's stomach churned. What if the girl asked questions? How could she explain?

Lucas laughed. "I'm fine right where I'm at."

"Fine." Kaitlyn rolled her eyes. "I'm sure we'll have a chance to talk when we get our spa treatment. I can't wait to hear all the details."

*Like grandmother, like granddaughter.* Pulling off this charade might be harder than she thought. Part of her felt guilty for trying to pull the wool over his family's eyes. What would they think of her if they knew she was an imposter?

She'd always prided herself on telling the truth.

Then there was Heather sitting in their hotel room, working furiously while Megan sat in a restaurant getting a free meal. Maybe she should bring back the leftovers to clear her conscience.

Grandma Ruby reached for her cane and stood. "I would like to make a toast." She lifted her water glass high in the air. "To Lucas and Megan. May you listen to the Heavenly Father as He guides you in your relationship."

Megan didn't know whether to join in the toast or run to her hotel room. Lying was wrong. This relationship with Lucas, if she could call it that, was doomed from the start.

Lucas set down his fork. He hadn't eaten a meal that delicious in a long time.

Grandma Ruby signed the receipt and tucked her copy in the neckline of her dress. "I'll see you all for breakfast at eight a.m. sharp in the Ocean Club room. Remember, I signed everyone up for kayaking, so dress appropriately."

Megan sucked in a breath and released it slowly. Was it the early morning or the thought of kayaking that made her squirm in her seat?

"And spa treatments, right, Grandma?" Kaitlyn smiled.

"Yes, we'll pamper ourselves in the afternoon." Grandma Ruby nodded.

The adults excused themselves from the table.

"Who wants to play Balderdash?" Jacob asked. "You know you want to, Lucas. You're the best fibber out of all of us."

Lucas's jaw clenched. The game called for bluffing definitions of words in hopes the other players would guess the answer as the true dictionary definition.

Kaitlyn ribbed his side. "Yeah, remember the time you made up a definition for collywobbles?"

How could he forget?

"I've got to hear this." Megan rested her elbows on the table and leaned in.

"A collie's first steps after waking from surgery." Kaitlyn laughed. "Can you believe we voted for that one?"

Megan nodded. "Sometimes the best answers are the simple ones."

Lucas didn't know if his sudden bellyache, the real definition of collywobbles, was from the rich dinner or knowing everyone thought he was a good liar. Either way, he wasn't about to prove them right or wrong by playing a game of Balderdash. "I think Megan and I are going to call it a night."

"Oh, I get it." Jacob smirked. "You and Megan want to be *alone.*"

Heat rose up his neck. Being alone with Megan was against what he'd promised. He wouldn't want to go back on his word and send Megan running before his grandma's birthday bash. "Think whatever you want. I had a late surgery yesterday and I'm tired."

"Is the animal okay?" Megan's concern warmed his heart.

"It was a Boston Terrier—ruptured his anterior cruciate ligament. He made it through surgery just fine."

"Well, if you two aren't going to play Balderdash, then I'm headed to bed." Kaitlyn pushed her chair back, stood, and left.

Lucas gestured toward the door. "Megan, I'll walk you to your room."

"See you later. Think I'll hang out here awhile." Jacob grinned. "You never know who I might meet."

Lucas understood completely. He'd been at the hotel only a short time before his and Megan's paths crossed. Now, they walked to the elevator in silence and stood a comfortable distance away from each other waiting for the doors to open.

"I don't think I can do this." Megan broke the quiet.

"What do you mean?" He feigned ignorance.

"Us. Pretending we're an item when we're not. I feel like such a hypocrite. You saw the way your family looked at us, and your grandmother's toast ... "

He took a step towards her. "We haven't said anything that is untrue. Let them think what they want. It makes my grandmother happy."

"But don't you feel the least bit guilty?"

"Part of me feels uneasy, but it's not like we've made any promises to them or each other."

The elevator doors opened. Megan stepped inside.

"Will I see you in the morning?" Lucas rocked back on his heels, tucking his hands inside his pant pockets.

Megan shrugged, the confusion in her eyes not giving him an ounce of hope. She pressed an elevator button and the doors closed.

Would he ever see her again? The bigger question was what would he tell his family in the morning? He pushed down his frustration, walked down the hotel corridor into the main lobby.

"Lucas?" A woman called to him. "What are you doing here?"

*Uh-oh.* He'd know that voice anywhere. Things were about to get more complicated!

# CHAPTER FIVE

Megan let herself into her hotel room and found her sister fast asleep. Papers littered the bed all around her, her laptop was open, the screen dark. Poor Heather. She wasn't having much of a vacation.

Megan quietly slipped off her sandals and shrugged out of her sweater.

Tonight hadn't ended well. She'd challenged Lucas with her questions and, by the shocked look on his face, disappointed him as well. What did he expect? That she'd continue with his plan even if it hurt his family in the long run? No free vacation was worth her reputation.

Maybe she was giving herself too much credit. What were a few days in the scheme of things? Lucas's family wouldn't miss her when this whole thing was over. Chase's family never tried to contact her after they broke up. So what did it matter?

Truth was she'd enjoyed the dinner with Lucas's family. His parents smiled at her from across the table. Kaitlyn was friendly and outgoing, Jacob too. He joked with her about his calamari having legs and complimented her sweet nature in a non-flirtatious way. Why was she taking this arrangement so seriously? Why couldn't she simply have fun? Wasn't that why she'd come in the first place? Lucas didn't seem bothered by the deception. So why should she?

If she was honest with herself, it was the thought of kayaking that put her on edge. Part of her wanted to try it, and yet…

"Meg, are you here?" Heather's groggy voice floated across the room.

"Yes, I'm back."

"What time is it?" Heather covered a yawn.

"Eight o'clock. It's still early if you want to grab a bite or something." She sat across from her sister on the bed.

If Megan had her way, she'd stay put.

Heather pushed herself to a seated position. "Can we order room service? I look a mess and would rather not get out of my sweats and re-do my makeup."

Megan released a breath. "I already ate, but order anything you'd like. Want to watch a movie while we wait?"

"I'm afraid I'll fall asleep again. I didn't realize I was so exhausted. Thank you so much for inviting me. The quiet room and sound of the surf is exactly what I need to relax." Heather perused the room service menu. "Wish I was able to spend time with you, though, instead of focusing on work. I hope you're not going to be bored."

Megan stood and walked over to her suitcase and pulled out a pair of pajamas. "Don't worry about me. I'll find plenty to do."

Heather didn't need to know how she'd bumped into Lucas, agreed to pose as his girlfriend, and how her trip had turned into an all-expenses-paid vacation. With what Lucas and Grandma Ruby had planned, Megan doubted she'd have a spare minute. That's if she was brave enough to join them.

"So what looks good to you? Order anything on the menu."

"You sure you can afford this place? The hotel lobby is incredible and it's oceanfront to boot."

"Just leave the bill to me, and don't worry about it. It's taken care of." Megan slipped into the bathroom to change into her pajamas before Heather could ask any more questions.

From the other side of the door, Megan heard her sister order an organic mixed green salad and Gracie's Rigatoni Mac and Cheese. Good choice.

As Megan readied for bed, her thoughts drifted to Grandma Ruby.

Lucas's grandmother was sweet, with plenty of spunk and charm. The woman had a special way about her that made others want to listen. Maybe it was her passion about life—and love. Megan couldn't blame her for wanting to see her oldest grandson married with a family. Anyone reaching her age would want that as well. Megan also couldn't blame Lucas for wanting to make his grandmother happy.

A knock sounded on the door. "Room service."

Megan donned the white robe hanging on the hook in the bathroom and went to answer the door, but Heather beat her to it. Her sister handed the worker two twenties and said, "Keep the change." She closed the door and shrugged. "I can't have you pay for everything."

Little did Heather know who was really footing the bill. Better not make a scene. Megan situated herself under the covers and relaxed under the weight of the downy comforter.

As Heather ate beside her, they watched an old television rerun of *I Love Lucy*.

"Know what we need?" Heather asked when the show was over.

Megan yawned. "What's that?"

"A good soak in the hot tub. According to this brochure, there's one on the top floor." Heather smiled.

What were the chances she'd run into Lucas or his family? Was it worth the risk? She couldn't deny her sister some pleasure while in Monterey.

"Now you're talking. Let's go!" Megan bolted out of bed and grabbed her bathing suit from her suitcase.

Ten minutes later, they were on the elevator.

"Are you sure you need sunglasses or that big sunhat?" Heather laughed and rolled her eyes.

"I'm trying to look the part of a woman on vacation." She struck a pose.

"Well, with that getup, no one will recognize you." Heather grinned.

*Perfect!*

They rode the elevator to the sundeck on the top floor with two whirlpool spa tubs and a fireplace. Surprisingly, no one else was there.

They removed their cover-ups and slipped into the hot tub closest to the glass railing and view. Lights dotted the landscape, and the sound of the whirlpool jets and surf added to the tranquil atmosphere.

"I could get used to this." Heather slunk a little deeper into the water.

Megan sighed. "Me too."

Just as they got comfortable, a hotel clerk told them it was closing time.

Megan furrowed her brows. "Sorry, Sis. Next time we'll look at the hotel schedule."

"Definitely." Heather dried herself with a towel and replaced her cover-up. "Speaking of which, you were gone a long time today. What did you do?"

Megan had avoided the topic ever since returning from dinner. How could she be honest and yet keep Lucas and his family a secret? At least for now.

"I got a lemonade and a bowl of clam chowder and sat on the deck until it was time for dinner, and then I ate at Schooners." There, she'd told the truth.

On the way back to their room, she carried her sunglasses and sunhat in hand. What a mistake!

Her eyes connected with Lucas's as they passed in the hallway. Guilt, and a bit of embarrassment, crossed his features.

He wasn't alone.

The gorgeous woman by his side had her hand neatly tucked inside the crook of his arm, absorbed in their conversation and captivated with Lucas. Her laughter floated down the corridor behind them.

Heather wrapped an arm around her shoulder. Concern etched her forehead. "You're thinking of Chase, aren't you?"

Megan placed her sunglasses on her face, covering up her jumbled thoughts and her sister's misdirected question.

"Okay. I won't bring him up now." Heather dropped her arm to her side. "But sometime during our trip I want you to talk about your feelings. You dated Chase a long time. And he got engaged so quickly."

Maybe she *was* angry with Chase.

Or maybe she was disappointed with Lucas. At least she hadn't given him six years of her life. It took him only an hour to find someone to replace her.

Lucas and Nicole rounded the corner.

"This place is a maze. Thank you for walking me to my room. It's been nice to catch up." She scanned her room key and the green light flashed.

"It won't seem that difficult in the morning. Good night." He smiled.

The second the door clicked shut, Lucas released a breath. Thank goodness she didn't invite him inside to continue their conversation, not that he would've accepted. One blind date was enough. He didn't know why Daniel ever thought they'd be a good match. While Nicole was smart and kind, she enjoyed climbing the corporate ladder. He, on the other hand, loved his job as a veterinarian but family was more important. He hoped to have his own brood one day and Nicole definitely didn't have that on her goals list.

What were the odds Nicole's room would be on the same floor as Megan's? He rounded the corner in time to see Megan and her sister slip inside a room at the far end of the hall.

Megan had looked completely stunned when she'd passed him and Nicole. If only he could've stopped so he could explain. Megan already had doubts about joining his family in the morning, and now it would take a miracle for her to show up.

Why would she after what she'd seen? Truth was, he was only trying to be a gentleman, nothing more. Nicole had a persuasive way about her. A chance meeting outside the hotel and he knew he was in for a long conversation. Why had he allowed himself to get sucked in? Grandma

Ruby, that's how. She'd taught him how to listen and be respectful. Look where that got him.

He ran a hand through his hair and walked down the hallway, his head bent. He nearly bumped into Megan.

She clutched an empty ice bucket to her chest.

They sidestepped the same direction and back again.

"Excuse me." Her voice held a hint of annoyance.

He held up a hand. "Can we talk a minute?"

"Why would we need to talk?"

He motioned her down the hall toward the ice room. "Nicole and I went on one date three months ago. She's here on business. I ran into her in the hotel lobby. She asked me to help her find her room because she's directionally challenged. I walked her to her room and left—"

"You don't owe me an explanation. We don't even know each other."

"But I'd like to know you. And I'd like for us to keep our arrangement."

"Sure you wouldn't rather invite Nicole? She seems smitten."

Was Megan disappointed? She certainly didn't sound jealous. "Positive. My family has already met you. I can't hardly show up with a different woman tomorrow. Besides, Nicole and I have different views on life."

Megan cocked her head. "And how do you know *we* don't?"

The only way to answer that question was to ask questions. "Do you love kids?"

"Of course. I'm a teacher."

"Do you need a six-figure income to be happy?"

She crinkled her pert nose. "Of course not."

"There's your answer. Nicole and I want different things in life. End of story. Now, will you please come kayaking with my family tomorrow?"

Megan hesitated.

"Please?" Lucas lowered his voice.

Megan's brows lowered. "How do I know you're telling me the truth?"

"Guess you're going to have to trust me on this one." Lucas stepped a bit closer. "Even if we didn't have this arrangement, I wouldn't have asked Nicole. One date with her was enough for me."

Megan pressed her lips together as if contemplating her decision. He didn't know much about her, but he was learning she was the type of woman who followed her convictions. Would she be able to continue with this charade? Should he?

Her forehead creased. "I've never kayaked before."

"Don't worry. It'll be great. I'm sure they'll give us thorough instructions before we step foot in the water."

She held back a smile and shrugged. "I have nothing better to do … "

He grinned. "So you'll come?"

She paused, then nodded. "Okay, I'll come."

"Great!" He hadn't expected her to agree. There were so many reasons for her to say no, but he wasn't going to question it. "See you for breakfast at eight."

On his way to his hotel room, his steps felt light. Who knew his chance encounter with Nicole would end up helping him secure another date with Megan. He chuckled. But *were* there any chance encounters with God? He didn't think so. Felt more like a divine appointment.

A niggling grabbed at his gut. Megan wasn't his girlfriend, and pretending she was wasn't honest. But seeing his grandmother happy was the best birthday gift he could give her—as long as she didn't find out the truth.

# CHAPTER SIX

Kayaking was a new adventure and one she approached with more than a little trepidation. Still, Megan was determined to be brave and she dressed prepared to get wet. She stepped out of her hotel room wearing flip-flops, exercise pants, and her favorite long-sleeved rash guard over her bathing suit. She'd pulled her hair back in a ponytail, and a baseball hat and sunglasses shaded her eyes.

She was to meet Lucas and his family at the Ocean Club room at eight before their kayaking reservation. Her stomach fluttered and not only because of the kayaking. Lucas was adamant he and Nicole weren't right for each other. How did he know after only one date? She'd known Chase had dreams of a high-society life for years, and yet she'd hung onto their relationship for as long as she could before breaking it off. Truthfully, he probably would've ended it if she hadn't. She wished she was as clear-minded as Lucas had been.

She glanced at her phone. There was just enough time to grab a cup of something hot at Tidal Coffee, the hotel's coffee shop. She hustled down the stairs and out the main doors to the deck of the plaza.

The cool ocean breeze hit her and sent a shiver down her spine. She hoped the weather would warm up before it was time to kayak. She expelled a breath into her hands and rubbed them together. A cup of coffee was just what she needed.

Opening the door to the coffee shop, she nearly rammed into a woman holding a cup of something hot in her hand. Disaster averted!

It took her a second to realize she was the same woman who had clung to Lucas's arm last night. *Nicole, was it?*

"Watch where you're going!" Nicole glared at her.

"I'm sorry. I need to slow down."

Nicole's eyes softened. "I hope you're not in too big of a hurry. There's a big party waiting to order."

Megan spotted Lucas and his family in line, everyone except for Grandma Ruby. It gave her a bit of pleasure to know Nicole was on her way out the door.

"I'm with them." Megan nodded Lucas's direction.

Nicole's brows cinched closer. "You know Lucas?"

"I do." She couldn't get herself to say anything more—or ask Nicole the same question.

"How?" Nicole wouldn't let her off the hook.

She swallowed hard. Could she say it? "We're dating."

"Really?" Nicole looked her up and down. Apparently she didn't like what she saw. Or maybe she was assessing her competition.

Megan had to walk away from the woman before she blew their cover. "Excuse me. Have a good day."

"Look who's here!" Kaitlyn called, nudging her big brother's shoulder.

Megan gave a small wave to Lucas and his sister, then glanced over her shoulder at Nicole, but the only thing she saw was the door swinging shut and the fiery redhead retreating through the glass.

Now maybe Nicole would leave Lucas alone. *One could hope!* If Megan was to continue this charade and get her free vacation for the week, she didn't need another woman getting in the way.

Lucas grinned at her. "Just in time for me to buy you a cup of coffee. Kaitlyn, you and Jacob won't mind if she cuts in line, right?"

She stopped him with a hand. "It's okay. I'll wait my turn."

"No, it's fine. Right, Jacob?" Kaitlyn asked.

Jacob's head hung down, buried in his cell phone. "What'd you say?"

Lucas laughed. "Megan, come on up here. Jacob wouldn't know it if a bomb went off."

"What about me?" Kaitlyn asked.

He wrapped his sister in a bear hug. "You're as sweet as the mocha I'm going to buy for you." He released his hold on the girl and rubbed her head with knuckled fingers.

"Thanks, bro." Kaitlyn scrunched up her face and scooted away. "I like the hug better."

Now it was Megan's turn to laugh. Lucas had a fun relationship with his siblings, and it was entertaining to watch. She had always wished for a brother, but her parents had stopped after two children. Her dad never complained about not having a son, and neither did her mom.

"I'm sure Megan likes your hugs too." Kaitlyn winked.

"Of course she likes hugs," Lucas answered. "But we're not into PDA." The look he gave her pleaded with her to play along.

His words grabbed Jacob's attention. "Not even hand holding?"

She didn't have a problem when two people held hands or hugged in public. Should she interject? No. It was more amusing to watch Lucas squirm.

Lucas continued. "Listen, little brother, I think I can manage my own love life, thank you very much." He almost sounded convincing. "Now cut it out. You're making Megan feel uncomfortable."

*Good save.* Although she wouldn't object if Lucas wanted to hold her hand. The truth of that surprised her. Shocked her, really. After all, he was still a stranger.

At the moment she'd be satisfied with the warmth of a hazelnut latte.

Good thing, too, because they were next in line.

*Nice digs.*

Lucas took in the view of the Ocean Club room after a breakfast of scrambled eggs, bacon, and croissants. He agreed with his mom. The blue walls and ornate rug added to the comfortable atmosphere. Reminded them of the home he grew up in.

When Megan excused herself to the ladies' room, he stepped out onto the balcony. The surf pounded below, and sea lions barked in the background. This place fit his grandmother's personality. She was strong like the ocean, and claimed her territory like a sea lion.

Grandma Ruby joined him on the balcony. "I like her."

Lucas wrapped an arm around her shoulder. "I'm glad you approve."

"But I wasn't born yesterday." She looked up at him and quirked a brow.

Heat rushed to his neck. "What do you mean?"

"You forced that girl to meet us. I can see how uncomfortable she is."

Little did his grandmother know the full truth of that statement.

"It's always uncomfortable to meet someone's family, especially for a big event like this. It's not every day your grandma turns eighty." He smiled, attempting to take the conversation on a new path and lighten the mood.

"Stop reminding me how old I am." She swatted at his hand resting on her shoulder. "We are just going to have to work extra hard to make Megan feel loved and part of this family. I can tell she's holding back. It's as if she doesn't trust us."

If only his grandmother understood what really had transpired in the last twenty-four hours. Personally, he thought Megan was doing a great job, but he'd comply to make his grandmother happy. "What do you have in mind?"

"You need to be more attentive. First we find out she's allergic to strawberries, and now we learn she doesn't eat eggs. You need to pay attention to these things. Makes a girl feel special."

Nothing ever got past Grandma Ruby. Why did he ever think he could pull this off?

She looked up at him, the quizzical expression back in her eye. "How long have you known this girl—"

"Mom, we need to get going. Our kayak reservation is in twenty minutes."

*Saved by his father.* "Thanks, Dad. We're coming."

"Lucas?" Grandma pushed him to answer.

"Long enough to know she reminds me of you." He kissed her on the cheek and held up his arm to lead her inside the Ocean Club room to join the others

She grabbed hold and squeezed. "Then show her how much you care."

His grandmother's words replayed in Lucas's mind all morning as the family donned waterproof pants and life vests, and tucked their cellphones in waterproof pouches.

*Pay attention and make her feel special.*

He could do both of those things without making it awkward, couldn't he? All he needed was a little creativity.

The instructor directed everyone to stand in a circle, then held up an oar and demonstrated how to row. "Grip your oar this way, and remember to scoop and not jab the water. Most importantly, remember to have fun."

Lucas stood next to Megan and leaned close. "Are you nervous?"

She chewed her lip. "Can you tell?"

"A little, but don't worry. I'll make sure we don't capsize. They say that rarely happens—"

"Rarely? With my luck … "

He rested a hand on her arm. "There's no such thing as bad luck. Trust me."

Her eyes rested on his and she let out a nervous breath. "Okay, we can do this."

"You bet we can." Was he talking about their relationship or kayaking? Felt like he'd taken a step forward on both counts. Maybe it was because it wasn't only her eyes that rested on his, it was the way she gripped his hand, as if she counted on his strength to pull her through. The smile she passed his way was nice too.

"Let me know if you'd like a single kayak or one for two," the instructor said, interrupting the moment.

"Megan, want to double up with me?" Kaitlyn asked. "You know, girl power and all."

Megan looked from Kaitlyn to Lucas and back again. "Well, I ... "

"She wants to ride with me, of course," Lucas wrapped a protective arm around her shoulder.

"Oh, come on." Kaitlyn folded her arms. "Can't you two do anything apart?"

Megan hesitated. "It's just that ... "

"She needs my rowing skills," Lucas said.

"And apparently she needs you to finish her sentences as well. C'mon Lucas. Let your girlfriend talk."

"Yes, Lucas, let your girlfriend speak." She poked his side with an elbow.

*She called herself my girlfriend.* A smile tugged at his lips. "Trying to help is all."

"Kaitlyn, I'd love to double up with you, but ... " Megan cleared her throat. "I'm scared. I almost drowned in a rushing river when I was seven. My dad had to rescue me."

"Oh, wow. I didn't know." Kaitlyn's features softened. "Lucas, you could've warned us this morning before Megan showed up for coffee. Now I feel like a jerk."

*You and me both.*

Megan shrugged. "No worries, really. I'll be fine. Just a little scared is all."

"Think I'll go ask Jacob before he goes by himself." Kaitlyn took off after her brother.

"You sure you want to do this?" Lucas lowered his voice.

Megan cocked her head. "Don't they say you have to get back on the horse?"

"More like get back in the boat." He grinned.

Her nervous laughter filled the air. "At least I'll *have* a boat this time."

"True," he said. "Shall we go?"

She squeezed his hand. "The only way I'll get in the kayak is if I go with you."

Why did that statement make him feel like the most fortunate man on earth?

Megan sat in the front of the kayak with Lucas behind her. The instructor had taken them to the beach and helped them launch. At first, they had to paddle hard to get out over the waves, but it got easier once they were in the bay.

Lucas reminded her that the instructors kept track of who was out in the water, and whether someone needed help. "Let me know if you are tired of paddling."

"I will." Her voice shook.

When she left her room that morning, she had no clue all those feelings of being a seven-year-old child would flash in front of her. She'd almost drowned in a river, not the ocean, and kayaking was far from flailing in the water without a paddle. If it weren't for her dad, she wouldn't be here right now. Even so, her father couldn't stop them from floating a hundred yards down the river. But he wouldn't let her go. It was an odd sensation of feeling scared, yet safe. In her dad's arms, she knew she would be all right.

*Is that the same with you, God? Am I going to be okay even though Chase has moved on and I feel like I'm drowning?*

Lucas gestured to the right with his oar. "Look, an otter."

Just as he said, she spotted the otter. He was on his back with something to eat between his paws. "Let's get closer."

"All right, but not too close. Remember what the instructor said."

Yes, she did. They were to be careful and respectful of the wildlife. Otters were curious little creatures and the kayakers weren't to engage with them. But they could get closer and take a picture. That was, if she was brave enough to get her phone out.

A few strokes to their right and the otter was within ten feet of them. Close enough. She reached into her pouch and pulled out her phone.

"I'll turn us around so you can get a picture with all of us in it," Lucas said.

She'd love a picture of the otter, but it had to include Lucas. If it weren't for him, she wouldn't have had the courage to be out in the water. She raised the cell phone with cold, wet fingers. "Say otter!"

He grinned as she snapped the picture.

# CHAPTER SEVEN

When Megan entered her hotel room, Heather was jumping up and down as if she'd won the lottery. She hugged Megan, then rested her hands on her shoulders. "Mr. Carmichael is pleased with my work and told me to take the afternoon off. We can do anything we want. A spa treatment, the Monterey Aquarium, shopping, whatever we want to do."

*A spa treatment with Lucas's family would have to wait.* The last thing Megan wanted was for Heather to find out she'd been playing the part of girlfriend to handsome Lucas Hunter. She'd never hear the end of it. Her sister would think she'd gone crazy, for sure. But if she didn't show up, Kaitlyn would be disappointed. So would she.

"Really?" Megan asked. "That's great."

Heather stopped bouncing. "Then why don't you sound excited?"

"Just tired is all. I'm a bit sore from all the paddling."

"I'm surprised you got into the water. Get any pictures?"

"You and me both. It took everything I had to get into that kayak, but the instructors were super helpful, and the guy I shared a kayak with spotted an otter. It was amazing!"

"The guy or the otter?" Heather teased.

*Definitely the guy.* Megan shrugged her off. "The otter, of course."

"Well, you did it, and I'm proud of you. Say, I wonder if the Vista Blue Spa has any openings this afternoon. I could really use a massage." Heather rubbed her neck.

With Lucas's big family taking up slots in the schedule, Megan doubted there would be any appointments available. "Let me get changed, and I'll go down to the front desk and check for you."

Heather picked up the hotel brochure. "The number is right here. I'll give them a call."

Before Megan could object, Heather punched in the number. A minute later, she set down the receiver, a glum look splayed across her face. "It's full this afternoon. Just my luck."

"There's no such thing as bad luck." Megan repeated Lucas's words. "You never know. People change their minds. Things happen."

Heather nodded, but her expression told Megan all she needed to know. Her sister was not happy and wanted— no, *needed*—a massage.

Megan grabbed a change of clothes out of her suitcase and went to the bathroom to shower and change. She had just enough time to hunt Lucas down before they were all to meet at the Vista Blue Spa. One way or another, she was going to make sure Heather would get a massage.

But what excuse would she give her sister for leaving?

The instant she turned off the hot water from her shower, an idea sparked. Of course! She dried herself off with a fluffy white towel, ran a comb through her hair, and quickly dressed.

When she opened the door, she found Heather sitting in the corner of the room, reading a book.

"Why don't you call the kids while I go figure something out."

The corners of Heather's mouth turned up in a sly grin. "Sounds mysterious."

*If I can pull this off, it will be.* Megan smiled. If only Heather knew what the real mystery would be. "I'll be back soon. Tell your family hello."

Before Heather could ask questions, Megan stepped out of their hotel room. She leaned her head against the door and swallowed the knot lodged in her throat. Would Lucas go along with her plan? Could they risk it?

Lucas flipped through the television channels in his hotel room.

He had thirty minutes before his scheduled massage with his family. He'd never had one before and looked forward to releasing some of the tension in his knotted muscles. Besides the usual tightness from his veterinarian job, hanging out with his family added to his stress. No, he couldn't blame them for the knots in his shoulders and neck. He'd done it to himself. If he would've told Grandma Ruby the truth about Megan, he might not need that massage. But as it stood, thirty minutes couldn't come fast enough.

He turned off the television and flopped back on the bed.

Thoughts of his dog flitted through his mind. He missed Goldie. She was a great companion and a good listener to boot. The bed at the hotel seemed huge without his dog beside him. He picked up his phone and called Daniel.

On the third ring, Daniel picked up.

"Let me guess, you're missing your girl." Daniel's voice held a hint of laughter.

"How'd you know?" Lucas said. "Just calling to see how she's doing."

"Crying all day and night," Daniel teased. "When did you say you were coming to get her?"

"I'll be by right after Grandma Ruby's party on Saturday afternoon," Lucas said. "I'll text you when I leave the hotel."

"Perfect. Seriously, though, Goldie's doing great. No rush," Daniel said.

A knock sounded on the door, interrupting their conversation.

"Got to run! Give Goldie a belly rub for me." Lucas hung up the phone and went to answer.

The rapping sound continued.

"Coming!" He looked through the peephole and found Megan in the hallway. He opened the door.

She pushed her way into his room and told him to shut the door.

He smiled, then just as quickly knit his brows. "What's going on?"

"I have to talk to you about something important." She rubbed her hands together and paced the room.

Was she going to tell him to forget the whole thing? That she couldn't pretend to be his girlfriend any longer?

"The front desk staff wouldn't give me your room number, even after your uncle Robert walked by and told them I was your girlfriend. So Robert pulled me aside and told me." She winced. "Sorry about that. We really need to exchange phone numbers."

He let out the breath he was holding. "We can exchange numbers. Oh, I get it. You want to send me the otter photo." His attempt to lighten the mood fell flat. By the way she nibbled her lower lip something else was bothering her. "Did I do something wrong?"

"No, it's not about you. It's my sister. Heather's boss gave her the afternoon off, and I'd like her to take my place this afternoon at the Vista Blue Spa. I feel guilty that I'm having a great vacation and she's stuck in the room working."

He took a step toward her and smiled. "You're having a great vacation, huh?"

"Grandma Ruby has been generous—dinner at Schooners, breakfast in the Ocean Club room, kayaking, and now a spa treatment. I couldn't have planned it better myself."

Was it all about Grandma Ruby or did he have anything do to with it?

Megan narrowed her eyes. "But I can't in good conscience keep doing all these things when Heather is finally getting a break. Besides, what do I say to her? That I'm getting a massage when clearly she's the one who needs one? I can't do that to her."

"What do you want me to do?" Lucas asked. "It's a closed session. Grandma Ruby paid for all the rooms."

"I thought about that." Megan tapped her chin. "Please tell your grandmother that as much as I'd love a massage, what I really need is a nap."

*A nap?*

"But you and Kaitlyn have been talking all morning about how you can't wait to get a massage."

"But my sister—"

"Can join us. We'll make it work."

"How? She doesn't know about you or your family. It would blow both of our covers. Are you ready for that?"

"It will all work out. You'll see." He rested a hand on her arm. "If you and your sister show up a few minutes late, I'll have it all taken care of. Trust me."

Fact was, he didn't see why she would trust him. They'd built their relationship on false pretenses, and he would need to mislead his grandmother once again. Was it worth it?

After he and Megan solidified their plan, she left his room, promising never to barge in ever again.

Truthfully, he didn't mind.

# CHAPTER EIGHT

Megan glanced at the clock in her hotel room every few minutes, waiting for the time she and Lucas had agreed upon. "Time to go," she said at 3:05 p.m.

Heather grabbed the striped beach bag. "Are you going to tell me where we're going? And what's in this bag?"

"No, I'm not. But believe me, you're going to be thrilled." Megan hoped she'd be able to keep that promise and that the whole thing wouldn't blow up in her face.

Her heart beat a staccato rhythm on the elevator ride and as they walked down the hotel corridor toward the Vista Blue Spa. Would they run into Lucas or his family?

"You seem a bit on edge. Sure you want to do this— whatever we're doing?" Heather asked.

"I'm sorry, of course I do. It's you I don't want to disappoint."

"How could you disappoint me? I've been dying to get out of that hotel room, and that's exactly what we're doing."

The spa was in front of them now. No Grandma Ruby or Hunter family member in sight. Megan released a breath. Maybe this would turn out as relaxing as she'd hoped.

"We're going here?" Heather's eyes widened. "But I thought they were full."

"I've got connections." Megan laughed it off as they entered and approached the front desk.

"You must be Megan." If the woman's glowing skin was the results of spa's beauty treatments, they were in for a treat. "Follow me, please."

She led them into a private room with two massage tables. Soft music played in the background, and the lighting was dim and soothing. The receptionist gave them instructions and left.

"Tell me your secret. How did you get us in?" Heather asked.

*Lucas.*

Lucas arranged it all—the timing, the welcome, the private room. He had made sure both she and her sister would have a massage even though this was a private party for Grandma Ruby. A warm feeling rushed through her.

"Let's not waste time." Megan changed out of her clothes, then slipped under the sheet on her massage table, lying on her belly.

Heather did the same. "Megan, you're the best! Thank you."

"Tell me that after we're through." She giggled. "I've had massages that left me more sore than when I went in."

There was no need to fear. The massage therapist worked her muscles with just the right amount of pressure, and the scalp massage and warm aromatherapy towels added to the peaceful experience. She had never felt more pampered.

By the end of the hour, a new resolve came over her.

No, it wasn't Chase who was lying on the massage table next to her. And the sooner she put that man and his upcoming wedding out of her mind, the better. This trip to Monterey was not the honeymoon she'd planned, but a new beginning. She hadn't felt this relaxed in a very long time.

After a quick rinse, they donned their bathing suits and climbed into the hot tub for a good long soak.

"Thanks again," Heather said as she slid a bit lower under the hot water. "You outdid yourself this afternoon. I don't know how you pulled that off, but I'm grateful. This last hour has made the trip worth it for me."

"Yeah, sorry you've been working most of the time this week." Megan positioned herself in front of a set of jets. The pulsing water kneaded the muscles in her back. "I feel a bit guilty for all the fun I've been having."

"Oh, please. I want you to have fun. We both can't be miserable." Heather grinned. "Honestly, even though I'm working, it's really nice to get away from the daily grind. I do miss my kids, but they are having a great time at my mother-in-law's house. She spoils them something rotten."

"We all need to be spoiled every now and then." Megan lay back against the headrest. She shut her eyes and allowed herself to drift into a dreamlike state in the soothing water.

Fifteen minutes went by without either of them saying a word.

The woman who had greeted them when they first walked in tapped Megan on the shoulder. "Ladies, sorry to interrupt. Another party is ready to come in now."

Heather didn't budge and her eyes were closed.

Megan saw urgency in the woman's tight smile and manicured brows.

"We'd better go." Megan climbed out and wrapped herself with a towel. She dug into her beach bag and pulled out her sunglasses and hat.

"Oh, no. Not that again." Heather laughed.

"What? Don't like my vacation look?" She struck another pose.

"More like a disguise. Personally, I want to run into someone I know. It's not every day I indulge in such luxury."

If only Heather knew the real reason she wanted to hide. If she read the woman's look correctly, Lucas's family was just around the corner.

Megan looped her hand inside the crook of her sister's arm. "All good things must come to an end. Let's hurry back to the room and figure out what we want to do next."

Lucas breathed a sigh of relief as he made his way to his hotel room after his massage. He'd pulled off quite the feat this afternoon. It wasn't easy to keep his family from running into Megan, but the bigger obstacle was convincing Grandma Ruby that Megan needed a private room for two, especially since Kaitlyn wasn't the one who would be joining her.

He stepped off the elevator and recollected his conversation with his grandmother.

"It doesn't make sense. Why would she need two massage tables?" Grandma had asked. Lines etched her forehead.

"For her and a friend. They need time to catch up." He made sure Grandma understood it was *his* idea and not Megan's. "You said I should be more attentive and do something to make her feel special, so when she told me her dear friend was here at the resort, I knew just the thing.

And I don't want anyone from the family bugging them. Don't worry, Grandma. It'll be my treat."

"That's sweet of you, Lucas. But I've already taken care of it and don't intend for you to pay me back."

The next time they were all together he hoped Kaitlyn wouldn't give Megan a bad time for ditching her and going against what they'd talked about all morning. The last thing he wanted was to paint Megan in a bad light.

"You'll understand after you get that degree and work full-time," he told Kaitlyn when she'd heard Megan wasn't coming.

His sister rolled her eyes and crossed her arms like a defiant toddler, but a nice massage had loosened her right up and a soak in the hot tub had raised her spirits. "We should make s'mores tonight and sit around a bonfire," she'd said as they left the Vista Blue Spa.

"After such a relaxing massage, I plan to retire in my room and go to bed early." Grandma Ruby waved them off.

After a final count, only the three siblings had wanted to stay up, unless Megan wanted to join them. Now that he had her phone number, he could text and ask.

Or he could leave her alone.

She probably wanted to spend more time with her sister. Maybe now that Megan had a taste of Monterey without him and his family, she might not want to continue their charade. He didn't have a hold on her and didn't have the right to expect her to stick with the plan.

Once back in his room, he showered and changed into jeans and a sweatshirt, preparing for the night ahead.

His phone buzzed.

He glanced at the text. Daniel had sent him a picture of Goldie.

*Nicole called me. How does Grandma Ruby like your new "girlfriend?" Guess Goldie is not your only girl. Glad you're taking my advice!*

Strange. Nicole must have seen the two of them together. But to call Daniel? Maybe she cared for him more than he'd thought. Lucas typed a quick reply.

*Thanks for the picture! Goldie looks great. GR is a peach, like always.*

No need to get into the details. Daniel could tease like no one else, and right now he wasn't in the mood for his friend's ribbing, but he did appreciate seeing a picture of his dog. She appeared happy stretched out on Daniel's sofa. He grinned.

Lucas stared at his phone. Speaking of his "girlfriend," he would enjoy Megan's company at the bonfire. She had said she liked chocolate. Who didn't like graham crackers and roasted marshmallows?

Before he could change his mind, he typed an invitation.

*S'mores tonight. Want to join?*

A few minutes went by with no reply.

He put his phone on the nightstand and picked up the hotel brochure. There was no doubt Monterey was a beautiful part of California, and his family was fortunate to have this time together along the coast. Sacramento was a good town to grow up in, but felt worlds away from the sand and surf. He had always loved the ocean and wildlife and might have become a marine biologist if he'd lived closer to the bay. As it turned out, being a veterinarian suited him fine. He couldn't complain about the life God had given him. The only thing that would make it better would be to find a woman to share it with.

Could Megan be that girl?

He flipped the brochure over. According to the rules, they wouldn't be able to make s'mores at the fire pits on the hotel's back deck and would have to go to a nearby beach.

His phone buzzed. Jacob.

*Count me out. I'll explain later.*

Typical Jacob. From experience, that could mean a whole host of things, but most likely had to do with a pretty girl he spotted at the hotel. Jacob made friends wherever he went.

A few minutes later, his phone buzzed again. Kaitlyn.

*Sorry, bro. Decided to climb in bed with Grandma and watch a chick flick. Hope you don't mind. Have fun with Jacob.*

His phone buzzed for the fourth time. His heart skipped a beat when he saw it was from Megan.

*Sure. When and where?*

He smiled, but just as quickly his grin faded. He didn't have the heart to tell her the bonfire was off. He doubted she would get in a car with him alone and drive to a nearby beach to make s'mores, but she might meet him on the hotel deck for a cup of hot chocolate. He typed a quick reply.

*Change of plans. Meet by the fire pits on the back deck in an hour.*

She replied.

*I'll be there.*

Why did the thought of seeing Megan again make his heart feel light?

# CHAPTER NINE

M egan stood by the hotel doors leading to the back deck and peered out. Lucas was the only one sitting in one of the rattan chairs surrounding the fire pit. Where was Kaitlyn? Jacob? Grandma Ruby and his parents? Was this a ruse to get her alone? Or had everyone made other plans for the night?

Truthfully, it might be nice to get to know Lucas better, away from his family. They had several more days before the birthday party. Why not learn more about him, if for no other reason than to make their relationship seem more believable?

She pushed open the door and walked over. Lucas looked comfortable in his jeans and sweatshirt, and she had to admit he made a striking image in the glow of the firelight. "Hi there." She took the seat beside him.

"No one else is coming." His voice sounded like a warning.

"That's okay." Megan smiled. "It'll be good to have time to get our stories straight. Without anyone's ears and eyes on us."

"Isn't that the truth?" Lucas chuckled low. "Although I'm going to have to renege on the promise of s'mores. The best I can do here is a cup of hot chocolate. I ordered two."

She shrugged. "Sounds perfect."

"So far I know you have an allergy to strawberries, hate eggs, and have a fear of water."

"That pretty much sums it up." She grinned. "Oh, don't forget I love a hazelnut latte. And hot chocolate, of course."

As if on cue, one of the hotel staff approached, carrying a tray with two mugs of hot chocolate with whipped cream swirled on top. "Your hot chocolates, sir. Hope you enjoy." He set the mugs on the tile surround in front of them.

"Wow! I'm impressed. You couldn't have timed that any better." She lifted a mug to her lips and took a sip.

Lucas glanced at her and chuckled.

Megan lowered her cup. "What? Did I say something funny?"

"No, you have a mustache ... " He pointed to his own lip.

She snatched a napkin and wiped her upper lip. "How embarrassing."

He grabbed his mug and drank from it, allowing the whipped cream to touch his nose. He looked at her and grinned. "No need to be embarrassed. It happens to the best of us."

She handed him a napkin. Felt good to joke around. They'd been concentrating so hard on pleasing his family that they hadn't had a chance to enjoy each other's company and become friends.

Could they be friends?

"I want to know more about you." Megan set her cup on the fire pit surround. "Are you a morning person or a night person?"

"Definitely morning. You?"

"Both. I'm a night person during the summer, morning person during the school year."

He nodded. "Makes sense. Are you left-brained or right?"

"Totally right-brained. I love being creative. What about you?"

"Left," he said. "I need to be analytical for my job."

From what she'd gathered, he worked close to her in Sacramento. In fact, she'd noticed his veterinary office on the way to her school countless times and thought that's where she'd take a pet, if she had one.

With her busy lifestyle, she'd considered a cat, one that would snuggle with her after work but could take care of itself during the day.

"What do you think about cats?" She took another sip, this time careful to keep the whipped cream in her mouth instead of all over her face.

"Cats are great. I work with them all the time. But for me, I'm partial to dogs. My dog, Goldie, is a golden retriever and as sweet as can be."

"Oh, that's right. You said something about her watching tennis on television and taking long soaks in the tub." She quirked a brow. "Is that true or were you just trying to be cute to gain my trust?"

"It's true. Goldie can follow the tennis ball on the big screen and loves her baths." He playfully nudged her arm. "Did it work?"

"I'm here now, aren't I?"

"And you haven't even met Goldie yet."

*Yet? Did that mean she could meet the dog in real life?* Why did that sound so appealing?

"Do you have a cat? Or are you thinking about one?" Lucas asked.

"I'm considering it. I get lonely living by myself." A couple of days ago, she would've never given him that information. Now, after spending time with him and his family, he seemed trustworthy.

Lucas rested an elbow on the side of his chair. "Cats can be good companions, although they have an independent streak. But a dog? There's a reason they're called man's best friend. Or woman's best friend." He winked, then turned serious. "A dog of any size is a good protector, and their bark will deter people with bad intentions."

Lucas was sounding like her sister Heather. She had suggested Megan get a dog for the past four months since she broke up with Chase.

Would his name always come to mind? She quickly pushed the thought away.

"If you want to pursue getting a cat or dog, just let me know. I'd be happy to help you find one that's a good fit."

Maybe he did want to be part of her life outside Monterey

Her insides warmed. Was that from the hot chocolate, the heat from the fire, or was it the thought of spending time with Lucas in her hometown? She glanced at his profile. His brown eyes, straight nose, and strong jawline pulled her in, but it was the caring way he spoke that attracted her more.

"Thank you. I'd like that."

"No problem. It's what I do." He finished off his hot chocolate and set his mug on the tile surround. "Now tell me more about what you do. You said you were a teacher?"

"Yes, I teach kindergarten. Right now I'm off for the summer. It's nice to get away and have a vacation—especially this week." Why did she let that slip? She hid behind her cup and drank the remaining hot chocolate.

Lucas didn't miss a beat. "So why did you choose this week? I'm not complaining. It worked in my favor." He shot her a grin.

She hesitated. How much should she say? She didn't have anything to lose by telling him about Chase. "This is the perfect week for a vacation because my ex-boyfriend of six years is getting married this Saturday." She leaned back in her chair and brought her knees to her chest.

Lucas eyed her, his expression warm. "In other words, you're not over him."

"I'm the one who broke off the relationship. He wanted something I couldn't give."

"And that would be?"

"To lose a part of myself. To only focus on *his* needs, *his* desires, *his* goals. I have dreams too." She sank lower in her chair.

"Of course you do. That would be a lot for anyone."

"Apparently Stephanie Whitcomb doesn't have a problem with it."

"Well, then, that's the type of woman he should marry." His tone was convincing.

She sat a bit straighter. "When you put it that way, maybe the two of them are meant for each other—"

"And you are meant for someone who supports and encourages you and your dreams."

She shook her head. "But it's not all about me. I want to support and encourage someone too."

"I know that firsthand. Okay, yes, you are getting an all-expense-paid vacation, but you're showing your selfless side by hanging out with me and my family."

"It hasn't been that hard. In fact, you've made it kind of easy." She grinned.

"Is that so?"

"Yes. And you've been pretty selfless too, giving my sister and me private massages. By the way, how did Kaitlyn handle it? Is she mad at me?"

His forehead creased. "A little."

"Oh, no!" She gritted her teeth. "What can I do for damage control?"

"How about if you sit with her during the surrey ride tomorrow? She's dying to spend time with you."

She nodded. "I will."

"So that means you'll come tomorrow?"

"Definitely." Megan stifled a yawn. "But right now, I'd better get going before Heather comes looking for me. She still doesn't know about you."

"I get it. No problem." He stood and Megan joined him. They walked inside to the hotel elevator. "Thank you for trusting me about—"

"Chase. Chase Donovan." Was it her imagination or did Lucas's jaw flex when she mentioned her ex's name?

The elevator door opened.

"Good night, Megan. See you tomorrow."

She stepped forward and gave him a quick hug before scurrying inside the elevator and pressing the button.

The elevator closed with Megan inside.

*Megan.*

Lucas couldn't stop the grin from spreading across his face. The embrace showed him Megan cared for him at least a little.

Most likely she was grateful to have a listening ear.

Was it his turn to talk about the past?

He tucked his hands in his pockets as he strode across the hotel lobby toward his room. The week would be over in a few days, but her opinion mattered more to him than he thought possible.

What had changed?

Hot chocolate. Whipped cream. Time alone.

The truth smacked him in the face. Megan was the type of woman he wanted to date once they were back home in Sacramento.

# CHAPTER TEN

The salesclerk from Adventures by the Sea pointed to a spot on the brochure map. "The coastal recreational trail is a paved bike path that hugs the coast and is a great way to reach the Monterey Bay Aquarium, Cannery Row, and Fisherman's Wharf."

Standing beside Megan, Lucas wanted to wrap an arm around her shoulder, but his siblings would get on him after what he'd said about public displays of affection. He hadn't crossed that line, and would have to wait for the right moment to show Megan just how much she was starting to mean to him.

Grandma Ruby thanked the clerk for the maps and paid for three surrey bicycles before turning to the group. "We need a young person for each surrey—that means Lucas, Jacob, and Kaitlyn will be in charge of picking the teams. Megan, I assume you'll want to ride with Lucas?"

"Actually, would it be okay if I go with Kaitlyn?" She smiled at his sister.

Kaitlyn squealed and sidled up to Megan. Apparently all was forgiven from the day before.

*Perfect. Just like they'd planned.*

The teams were decided one by one. Lucas chose Grandma Ruby and his dad, Jacob picked his mom and

Uncle Robert, and Kaitlyn decided Aunt Mary should join her and Megan.

As everyone got situated in the surreys, Lucas glanced over at Megan and his sister. Kaitlyn was talking a mile a minute, her hands gesturing this way and that. He chuckled. Maybe this was a bad idea. He knew how much Kaitlyn could chatter on about anything and everything. Including him.

"I have the perfect seat between my boys," Grandma Ruby said. "I'll just put my feet up and let you two muscle it out."

The trill of her laughter reminded Lucas of years past when his grandpa was alive. His pawpaw could always bring a smile to Grandma Ruby's face. The tall man had large muscles from his farming days. He had planted groves and groves of almond trees, which supported his family and made him strong, to boot. It'd been eight years since his grandfather's heart attack, a long time, but every now and again his grandma would say something to remind Lucas of his grandpa.

"Ready, son?" His dad interrupted his musings. "Let's get this surrey on the road." He gripped the steering wheel with white-knuckled fingers and set his feet on the pedals. "If we hurry, we can be first in line."

Personally, he'd rather ride behind Kaitlyn's surrey. It would be nice to keep an eye on the women, especially Megan. He had to admit, his pretend girlfriend was worming her way into his heart. His face heated at the thought.

Lucas settled in his seat and pressed hard on the pedals, propelling them forward.

Soon he and his dad were in a nice rhythm as they rode on the path that bordered the ocean. The weather was perfect, a balmy seventy degrees, and the surrey's canopy kept their faces from getting too much sun. The slight slope of the bike path made for a gentle ride.

"Say, that's nice of your girlfriend to ride with Kaitlyn," Dad said. "Mom and I had to remind her that Megan is here to spend time with whomever she pleases."

"I agree," Grandma Ruby said. "We all want to spend time with Megan, but we shouldn't pressure the girl. The last thing I want is for her to run away…"

"Like you think I've done in the past?" Lucas pumped his legs, his breath catching.

Grandma Ruby patted his hand. "I wasn't going to say it, dear—"

"You didn't have to, Grandma." Lucas stared at the path in front of him. "It's the running family joke—pun intended. But you've got me all wrong, I don't plan on going anywhere. I'm here for your birthday celebration. Megan is too."

As he said the words, he hoped they were true. Each outing was a question mark where Megan was concerned, but he'd enjoy her presence whenever she decided to join them. One day—or should he say one outing—at a time.

Laughter rose behind them and nipped at their wheels.

"Come on, girls, let's pass them!" Aunt Mary's voice boomed. "Pump, pump, pump!"

"Let's let them go ahead," Lucas said.

"Never!" His dad pumped harder, gaining speed. "C'mon, Lucas. Pump!"

"As long as we don't tip this thing over." Grandma Ruby held tight to each of their arms, her voice strained. "I don't want to spend my birthday in the hospital!"

Lucas should've known better than to choose his dad for the surrey ride. For the last thirty-five years, his dad had competed in bike contests. Why would he stop now? And if he thought his dad would mellow out with Grandma Ruby onboard, he thought wrong. He laughed. "C'mon, Dad. Lighten up. Let the women go by."

Dad slowed the pace. "Okay, you win."

"Thank you." Grandma loosened her grip. "This is supposed to be relaxing."

Dad laughed. "Says the only person not pumping."

Grandma Ruby straightened in her seat and jutted out her chin. "Says the only person who paid for these contraptions. If you'd rather I get off—"

"No, of course not," Dad said. "I'm sorry. I love it that you're here with us. And that you made this trip possible."

"And I'm going to be around for a lot longer," Grandma Ruby said. "The oncologist's office called this morning and the biopsy result came back negative."

"Praise God!" Dad said.

Lucas agreed. "That's great news!"

The women passed by in their surrey. Megan looked over and smiled, her long blonde hair flowing in the breeze. She was beautiful, and she made a pretty picture sitting beside his sister and aunt, as if she belonged with them— with him.

"Stop rubbernecking and keep pumping." Grandma Ruby nudged his side and winked.

"You have to admit, she's a trooper." Lucas laughed. "Kaitlyn and Aunt Mary aren't the quietest ones in the family."

"Nor do they mind their own business," Dad said. "Before the end of the ride, they'll have Megan sharing all her deepest secrets."

*Like the one about her not really being my girlfriend?*
And what would they tell Megan about *him?*
"Very funny, Dad. I'm sure they're just having fun."
Or so he hoped.

A couple of hours later, Megan stepped out of the surrey at the return spot at Adventures by the Sea.

Her legs wobbled like Jell-O. She didn't remember the last time she'd worked out, at least since she was on her own and didn't have a boyfriend to impress. She almost said as much on the surrey ride, but she stopped herself in time. Wouldn't Kaitlyn and Aunt Mary be shocked if they knew? Instead they went on and on about how she and Lucas were a perfect fit and how happy he seemed.

Truth was, she was happier this week than she'd been in a long time—mostly because there was no pressure to act or talk a certain way like in the last weeks with Chase.

Now instead of feeling angry and hurt, there was a feeling of distance, as if time was healing her wounds.

Lucas came up beside her and pulled her aside. "How was it?"

"The surrey ride or being with Kaitlyn and Aunt Mary?" She smirked.

"Both. Either. Or whichever one you'd like to answer." He stumbled over his words. Was he nervous? Since they'd begun this charade, he hadn't seemed jumpy until now.

Jacob's surrey returned with Mom and Uncle Robert.

"The ride was fun, and your sister and aunt are really sweet. They made me feel very welcome."

"No nosy questions?"

"Not one."

Lucas released a breath. "Thank goodness."

She gripped his arm. "But I almost let the cat out of the bag—"

"What cat?" Kaitlyn asked.

"Hey, I didn't see you there." Lucas bumped his sister's shoulder. "Stop sneaking up on us."

"I'm thinking of getting a cat." Megan covered her tracks. "Lucas is going to help me find one."

Jacob joined them.

"Really?" Kaitlyn furrowed her brows. "I know he's a vet and all, but he's more of a dog person."

"Yes, I know." Megan grinned. "He loves his Goldie."

"Have you seen her watch tennis on television?" Jacob's eyes widened. "She actually follows the ball."

Lucas wore an I-told-you-so expression.

Megan smiled. "She is one amazing dog."

"She sure is." Jacob agreed. "Lucas lets me take her on walks." He leaned in. "Goldie is definitely a chick magnet."

"She is, is she?" Megan glanced at Lucas.

His mouth dropped open and he lifted his hands in a don't-look-at-me gesture.

Kaitlyn rolled her eyes. "Jacob!"

Jacob stepped back. "Hey, what can I say? That dog loves me as much as I love her."

"So what's next, Grandma?" Kaitlyn asked.

"That's all I have planned for today," she said. "Go explore Monterey and have fun. Remember, tomorrow we're going to the aquarium."

After a few minutes of small talk, the family disbanded. His parents and grandparents headed back to the hotel. Uncle Robert and Aunt Mary went in search of clam chowder. And Jacob and Kaitlyn said they were going to collect shells at the beach, which left her and Lucas alone.

"Want to grab an ice cream? I saw a place down the street." He gestured.

"Yes," Megan said. "Something cold sounds good."

As they walked down the block toward the ice cream parlor, Megan spotted her sister coming toward them. She pulled Lucas into a nearby shop. If she had paid attention, she would've chosen an antique store or sock shop instead of a tattoo studio.

"May I help you?" A man greeted them. Tattoos covered his neck and arms.

"Just looking, thanks," Lucas said.

Megan kept an eye out for her sister through the window. Had Heather seen them?

"What do you think about this one?" Lucas pointed to a skull with octopus legs.

Megan smiled and shook her head. "No, thanks. Not for me."

Lucas grinned. "Not my style either." He lowered his voice. "Any sign of Heather?" Just as he said the words, her sister walked by the tattoo studio's window, talking on her cell phone.

*Phew!* Her sister's conversation had her complete attention. That thought brought a huge sense of relief.

But just as quickly guilt crept in. She was sneaking around with a guy she'd only known for three days—and yet it felt like they'd known each other for three months. Was that what it was like for Chase and Stephanie? Did four months seem like four years? Was that why their relationship moved so quickly? Was it possible?

Lucas closed the gap between them. "Hey, are you okay?"

"Yeah, just feel a bit deceptive is all. It's one thing when it's your family and another when it's my own. Know what I mean?"

"I know exactly what you're talking about. On the surrey ride, Dad and Grandma Ruby had nice things to say about you being my girlfriend. Doesn't feel right, does it?"

"No." Megan shook her head. "What should we do?"

"Let's get out of here and grab that ice cream. Cooling off will help us figure things out."

They thanked the tattoo artist for letting them look around, then left the studio. As they walked down the street toward the ice cream parlor, Lucas took hold of her hand.

As much as she told herself to pull away, her hand in his felt like the most natural thing in the world.

She was falling for him—and fast!

Impossible. As the song said, "You can't hurry love."

Once inside Frozen Bliss, Lucas ordered an ice cream sundae for them to share. They sat at a small bistro table by the window.

"When I asked you to pose as my girlfriend, I had no idea we lived in the same town." Lucas dug his spoon into the ice cream and took a bite.

Megan grinned. "Yeah, what are the odds?"

"I also didn't know if you were single."

"Or that my ex-boyfriend's wedding was this Saturday." Megan swiped at the whipped cream.

By Lucas's pinched expression, that last comment hit a nerve, but just as quickly he relaxed his features and sent her a tender smile. "Or that I'd really begin to fall for you . . . "

Megan dropped her spoon and held up a hand. "Please don't say it unless you really mean it, because I'm still recovering from a pretty deep hurt. Chase and I dated six years, and he's getting married after only knowing her for four months!" She couldn't hide her incredulous tone.

"Ah, I see." He leaned toward her. "You don't think two people can fall in love that quickly?"

"No. You can't hurry love. What's the rush anyway?"

Lucas leaned toward her. "After what you've told me about Chase, the last thing I plan to do is play with your heart."

She liked the sound of that. How had they gotten to this place so quickly? There was an ease between them that she never could have imagined when he'd first suggested this plan. "What do we tell your family? And Heather? She's been amazed that I've been able to keep myself busy all this time. Little does she know … "

"That you've been with me."

"And your family."

"Yes, my family."

They ate the remaining ice cream in silence, and parted ways no closer to figuring out the best way to approach telling everyone their relationship was a façade. But what if it wasn't? Suddenly it felt more real than ever before.

# CHAPTER ELEVEN

Lucas strolled through the Monterey Bay Aquarium with Megan and his family. They looked at the jellyfish and seahorses, and watched the staff feed the sea otters and African penguins. They also viewed a diver hand-feed the sharks, fishes, and other animals in the kelp forest exhibit. It was a beautiful day, and time with Megan was becoming more natural as each day passed. They filed into the auditorium to watch a film about white sharks, and the journey of gray whales, brown pelicans, and elephant seals.

The lights dimmed and the film began. Sitting beside Megan, his arm draped across the back of her chair, he started to feel like the boyfriend he was posing to be. If only it were true. Lucas's cell phone buzzed in his pocket. He took it out and glanced at the screen.

Daniel.

Lucas had told him that Grandma Ruby had a lot of things planned and Daniel shouldn't call unless there was an emergency. His heart rate quickened. He leaned close to Megan and whispered, "I've got to answer this."

She nodded, then turned back to the film.

Lucas slipped out of the dark room, the doors clicking behind him. He answered the call. "Hey, Daniel, what's up?"

"Ah, man, I hate to tell you this, but Goldie swallowed my pocketknife. I left it on the coffee table, and the next thing I knew, it was gone."

"You sure you didn't misplace it? What about Bruno? Your dog has been known to eat some strange things." Lucas's phone signaled low battery, and the cell reception wasn't good. *Not now!* "Hang on, man … I don't have much of a signal." He walked down the hallway and out the main aquarium doors. The sun hit him in the face. He walked to the side of the building covered in shade.

"No, it was Goldie. I saw it happen. Besides, Bruno has been with Kimberly all day. I'm getting in the car now to take Goldie to the pet hospital. You don't need to come, but I thought you'd like to know … "

This was definitely an emergency. If Goldie swallowed the pocketknife, she'd need emergency surgery to remove it. He trusted the other vets to do the surgery, and yet he wanted to be there with his dog. Goldie was his life, and he loved that dog like crazy. She was family.

He ran a hand through his hair, panic rising in his chest. "I'll meet you over there. I can be there in a few hours."

"But your grandma, and the rest of your family—"

"Will understand," Lucas said. "After I know Goldie made it through surgery, I'll come right back. The birthday party isn't until tomorrow."

"I'm sorry, dude. I never imagined she'd make a meal out of my pocketknife."

"And you're sure she ate it?"

"No doubt."

"Then I'm on my way. I'll meet you at the hospital." As they ended the call, his phone died. Why'd he forget to charge it last night?

After discovering the door he exited was locked, he rushed down the street toward the hotel. He could charge his phone in the car and let Megan and his family know where he'd gone. They knew how much he loved Goldie and wouldn't hold his hasty exit against him. He'd be back as soon as he could—not in time for dinner tonight, but definitely in time to celebrate Grandma Ruby's birthday tomorrow.

Once at the hotel, he dug in his wallet and pulled out the valet ticket for his car. The hotel employee took it and returned with his SUV. He got in and wound his way to the highway, heading north, before remembering to plug in his cell phone.

He dug in his console for the phone charger.

It wasn't there.

When the movie ended, Megan took out her cell phone from her purse and glanced at the screen. Nothing. No message from Lucas to let her know where he'd gone.

The rest of the family followed suit. No one had heard from Lucas.

"He got a phone call when the movie started." Megan attempted to ease their fears, hers included.

"I wondered what that was all about," his mom said.

"Probably a call from work," his dad said.

"Maybe he went back to the hotel," Aunt Mary chimed in.

"I know, he ran away from Megan. Right, Grandma?" Jacob laughed. "He runs from all his relationships."

"Jacob!" Grandma Ruby scowled. "We all know that's not true. I see the way he looks at Megan, and you do too. Let's give Lucas the chance to explain."

Grandma Ruby's words, and the tender looks the family sent her way, did nothing to boost her confidence. Yesterday's conversation at the ice cream parlor gave her the impression Lucas was falling for her. Was she wrong? She scrambled to find something to say.

"Lucas will get ahold of us, don't worry." Grandma Ruby gave her a tentative smile. "Tonight we're meeting at El Torito for dinner at seven. Please come."

Could she spend time with Lucas's family without him? She had not only grown close to Lucas, but his whole family as well. Would one more dinner with them make it more difficult to say goodbye?

Megan took a deep breath, and agreed. She walked away before she changed her mind and stepped inside the gift shop to look for a souvenir for Heather.

As she looked at the magnets and other small trinkets, she heard Lucas's aunt and uncle talking on the next aisle.

"I really thought Megan was the one." Aunt Mary tsked.

"Why can't Lucas commit?" Uncle Robert asked. "I hate to say it, but Jacob's right. Lucas has run away again."

Megan's stomach knotted. If anyone knew Lucas well, it was his family. Disappointment swelled inside. She picked an otter keychain off the shelf, and went to pay for it.

Twenty minutes later, she walked into her hotel room and gave her sister the keychain.

"Thank you for the gift. That's really sweet of you."

"I'm glad you like it."

"I'm in the mood for Mexican food tonight. You?" Heather tucked her laptop into her computer bag.

"Funny you should mention it..." Megan flopped back on her bed and rolled over on her side. "Because I was going to say the same thing."

"Great minds think alike. Maybe it's the sister connection."

She took a deep breath, determined to tell Heather the whole story—where she'd been and who'd she'd been with all week. No more secrets. "If it were true, your sister radar would've told you that I haven't been completely honest with you this week."

Heather's brows furrowed. "What are you talking about?"

Megan sat up and sighed. "Where do I start?"

"You've been acting a bit strange, but I chalked it up to Chase getting married this weekend."

"At first, I was down about it, but now I realize he wasn't the one for me. Lucas helped me see that."

"Lucas?" Heather blinked hard. "Who's Lucas?"

"The guy I met when we first arrived. We've been spending time together all week. His whole family is here. It's his grandmother's eightieth birthday tomorrow."

Heather grinned and rushed toward her. "And you're just now telling me this?"

Megan winced. "It's a bit complicated."

Her sister giggled. "Doesn't sound very complicated."

"Until you know that he asked me to pose as his girlfriend. His family doesn't know we'd only just met."

Heather's eyes widened. "He asked you to lie to his grandmother?" Her cheery tone vanished.

"It was either that or get lectured all week about why he isn't in a relationship. His grandma can be quite pushy."

"And now you think he's the one for you?" Heather cocked her head and crossed her arms, her eyes narrowing.

"I thought he was, but he left while we were at the aquarium. Honestly, I don't know what to believe. His family teases him about running from relationships, but yesterday he told me he was falling for me."

"I'd like nothing better for you than to be in a relationship when Chase gets married. But the sooner you realize this guy is just pretending, the better."

Megan shrugged. "You're right. It just hurts. I was so hopeful."

"I'm sorry, Meg." Heather sat beside her and gave her a quick hug. "Are you sure you're up for Mexican food tonight?"

"Definitely," Megan said. "I hear El Torito is good." With Heather by her side, she'd be able to tell Lucas's family the whole truth—that she was never Lucas's girlfriend, even though she wished with all her heart it were true.

# CHAPTER TWELVE

By the time Megan walked up to El Torito's doors, panic rose in her throat. "Let's go somewhere else. I don't feel like eating here."

Heather linked her arm in hers. "But we're at the restaurant now. Let's just go in."

"There's something I didn't tell you. Lucas's family is coming here tonight—"

"There she is!" Kaitlyn's voice rose behind her. "Megan, I'm so glad you came."

Megan had no choice but to introduce Heather to Lucas's family—everyone except Lucas.

"This is my sister, Heather Graham. She's in Monterey on business." She winked at her sister to play along.

"We didn't know your sister was in Monterey. How lovely." Grandma Ruby gave Heather a quick embrace. "Please join us."

Heather gave her the kind of look that said where-have-you-been-hiding-these-wonderful-people? Megan grinned, but her insides twisted. Why did she think this was a good idea? It wouldn't be fair to eat a meal with Lucas's family and then tell them that she and Lucas had been pulling the wool over their eyes all week. That wouldn't sit well.

It had been hard enough coming clean with Heather. Her sister thought Megan was desperate to be in a relationship by the time Chase got married. That wasn't the case. Although, the idea did lessen the blow.

Before Lucas's departure, she was starting to believe it could be done—that you *could* hurry love if it was right.

But where was Lucas? No one seemed to know. She couldn't help but think the worst—that he'd run away from her . . . and his family. What kind of man would leave before his grandmother's birthday?

The hostess walked toward them, menus in hand. "Your table is ready. Follow me." She led them to a large rectangular table with chairs for ten.

Grandma Ruby sat at the head of the table. "Heather, if you don't mind, I'd like Megan to sit here." She gestured to the chair on her right.

Kaitlyn sidled up to Heather. "You can sit by me. I want to know what you think of my brother."

The man her sister had never met.

The man who'd left without saying a word.

The man Megan was falling for.

Her heart pounded. She had to end this deception for Grandma Ruby and the family, but more importantly she had to end it for herself. The sooner she told everyone the truth, the better.

But all throughout dinner, the words wouldn't come.

Sure enough, Goldie had swallowed Daniel's pocketknife. Silly dog. She wasn't a puppy anymore, and yet she continued to be mischievous.

"Can you believe my dog?" Lucas stared at the x-ray on the light box in his office. "I'm grateful Dr. Young stepped in. He's one of the best surgeons. At least the blade wasn't open and there'd been minimal damage."

"Yes, it definitely could've been worse," Sarah, his middle-aged assistant, said.

"Was Goldie mad at me for leaving this week? She didn't have to go to such great lengths to bring me home to Sacramento." He joked.

"Now that you know she's going to be fine, you'd better get out of town before Goldie knows you're here," Sarah said. "You don't want to miss your grandmother's party."

"My family has no idea where I'm at, and I'm sure they think the worst."

Her eyes widened. "Your *family* doesn't know you're here?"

Lucas ran a hand through his hair. "Hey, I've been a bit distracted. The truth is I forgot my phone charger. Mind if I borrow yours?"

"Sure. I'll grab it from the break room." Sarah hustled out the door.

Lucas glanced at his watch. 7:15 p.m. Dinner time. He moaned and kicked himself for not getting ahold of anyone sooner. What must Megan think? She was adaptable, courageous, and sweet. Not just any girl would trust him enough to get onboard with his plan. True, she was trying to keep her mind busy and get over a wounded heart. But if her hand in his and their close conversation were any indication, she seemed open to starting a new relationship. And now he might have blown it.

Lucas had a lot of explaining to do. Megan deserved to be treated with respect and admiration. His family deserved the same treatment.

He picked up his office phone and left Jacob a message. He was the perfect person to give Megan and his family the news about Goldie. His brother loved the dog almost as much as he did.

Sarah returned to his office, charger in hand. He plugged it into the wall as well as his phone.

"Don't worry about Goldie," Sarah said. "We'll take really good care of her."

As soon as his cell phone charged, he looked in on Goldie one last time before heading out the double doors. If he hurried, he might be back in Monterey by midnight.

# CHAPTER THIRTEEN

F riday morning, Megan grabbed her clothes out of the hotel dresser drawer and set them in her suitcase.

"Are you sure you want to leave?" Heather asked from across the room. "My family doesn't expect me home until tomorrow—and I finally have some free time now that I'm done with work."

Megan zipped her suitcase. "I came here to get away from Chase and his upcoming wedding, and now being here reminds me of Lucas."

"We talked about it, remember?" Heather asked. "Your relationship with Lucas is based on pretense. His family is sweet, but I don't want you to get hurt. You've been through enough already, and you're vulnerable right now."

True, she was vulnerable, but it didn't have anything to do with Chase and his upcoming wedding. She was falling in love with Lucas. And now he was gone.

Someone rapped on their hotel door.

Heather went to answer it.

A hotel staff member handed her a note. "This is for Megan Conway."

Heather closed the door and pressed the note in Megan's hand.

"Will you read it?" Megan asked.

Heather scanned the piece of paper. "It's a note from Kaitlyn. Lucas must have arrived at the hotel late last night. Something happened to his dog, Goldie."

*Lucas is here?* The thought made her insides flutter. But Goldie... "Is his dog all right?"

Heather handed her the note.

*Goldie needed emergency surgery yesterday. She's okay. Lucas is in his hotel room asleep. See you at the party!*
*Kaitlyn*

A smile tugged at Megan's lips. So Lucas hadn't run away from her, as Jacob suggested. Yesterday Grandma Ruby tried to put it out of her mind, but she couldn't stop the negative seed from sprouting overnight. She glanced at her suitcase, all tidy and packed. Here she was, about to do the very thing Lucas's grandmother teased him about. And yet why hadn't Lucas called or texted her?

"I wonder what happened to Lucas's dog." Heather interrupted her musings.

From their conversations, she knew he loved that animal like crazy. "There's only one way to find out."

"The party?" Heather asked

"The party!" Megan whipped open her suitcase in search of her favorite dress.

The weather couldn't have been better for an outdoor lunch party on the promenade. The push and pull of the ocean as it lapped against the shore gave a relaxing, yet lavish, ambiance for Grandma Ruby and her guests. Besides the family, his grandmother had invited ten of her closest friends. Uncle Joe even showed up. Better late than never, although he only stuck around for a few minutes before he took off again.

Waiters walked around with napkins and appetizers for them to enjoy while they waited for everyone to arrive. An assortment of drinks, from iced tea and coffee to lemonade and soda, were available on the beverage table.

Lucas glanced around, looking for Megan. Why hadn't he personally let her know what happened? He could have gone to her room or texted after he charged his phone. Exhaustion, apprehension, a late arrival. All those things were true, and in the end he'd allowed Kaitlyn to let her know where he'd been.

"She'll be here. Don't worry." Kaitlyn stood next to him, a glass of lemonade in her hand. "You look so much better. I'm glad you listened to me and got more sleep."

"I feel better too. Yesterday was a crazy day."

He saw Megan then, walking down the outdoor steps that led to the promenade. Sunglasses hid her eyes—and her emotions. Was she happy to see him? Relieved he came back? Or was she mad at him for ditching everyone?

"There she is." Kaitlyn bumped his elbow. "And she brought Heather too."

How did his sister know Heather?

"Megan and Heather ate dinner with us last night," Kaitlyn answered, as if she'd heard his thoughts.

"Is that right?" He couldn't take his eyes off Megan as she descended the stairs. She was beautiful in her white summer dress that hit just above her knees. His eyes roamed down her shapely legs to her pink high heels. She made a striking image, and he liked what he saw.

"Dude. Close your mouth. You're gawking." Kaitlyn laughed.

Had he seen her only twenty-four hours ago? Felt much longer. He'd missed her. Was that crazy?

Megan must have spotted him when she reached the bottom of the stairs. Her gaze held his, and she removed her sunglasses. A smile lit her face as she made her way to him with her sister close behind.

"Wait a minute. Isn't this the guy we saw in the hallway? With the redhead?" Heather's tone was incredulous and loud enough for those around them to hear.

Before Lucas could say anything, Kaitlyn stepped forward. "What are you talking about? My brother isn't a cheat. You're acting like you've never met him before."

*Oh no! Had Heather blown their cover?*

Heather folded her arms. "I haven't."

Kaitlyn looked from Heather to Lucas. "What's going on?"

Megan shrugged. "We might as well tell her, Lucas."

"Tell me what?" Kaitlyn asked. "Lucas?"

"First of all, the redhead is someone I dated once. I saw Nicole in the lobby and she wanted me to help her find her room. End of story."

"Okay, but why is Heather acting as if she doesn't know you?" Kaitlyn asked.

Lucas cringed. "Promise me that you won't tell Grandma?" *What am I saying?*

"Sure, I guess…" By the uncertainty of Kaitlyn's tone, he didn't know if he believed her.

Megan jumped in. "Lucas and I met on Monday. He asked me to pose as his girlfriend for the week, and I agreed."

Kaitlyn furrowed her brows. "What? You guys aren't really a couple? You faked it this whole time?" Her voice rose with each question.

Lucas ran a hand through his hair. "Shh. Please. Not on Grandma's birthday."

Megan touched his arm. "It's okay, Lucas. They're bound to find out the truth."

His parents and Jacob came up beside them. Grandma Ruby, too.

"What's going on?" Dad asked.

"Lucas and Megan have been faking their relationship. They're not really dating." Kaitlyn didn't hold anything back.

Grandma Ruby gasped.

"I'm sorry." Lucas took hold of his grandmother's hand. "I wanted to tell you the truth all week, but the more time I spent with Megan, the more our relationship felt real." Lucas searched Megan's eyes. Did she agree?

"What's going on here?" Aunt Mary asked, clinging to Uncle Robert's arm.

"Nothing, that's what," Dad said. "Lucas, why don't you and Megan get something to drink? We'll entertain her lovely sister, won't we, Kaitlyn?" Dad's eyes bore into Kaitlyn's.

Why had he let this charade go so long? But was that what it was? Not in his mind. Not by a long shot.

Heather inched closer to Megan and clung to her. "I'm not sure that's a good idea."

Megan squeezed her sister's hand. "It will be fine. I promise."

"I'll take good care of her." Lucas wanted Heather to know she could trust him. That he had good intentions.

Mostly, he wanted Megan to feel at ease. He held out his hand and Megan took hold. He led her to the beverage station. She chose iced tea, and he poured himself a cup of soda. He pointed to the upper deck. "Want to get away from everyone?"

Megan nodded.

A few minutes later they stood against the railing overlooking the promenade and Grandma Ruby's guests.

"Sorry about yesterday—"

"How's Goldie?" Her smile warmed him.

"Fine now. She swallowed a pocketknife and had emergency surgery. I had to make sure she was okay. At first I wasn't able to call because I forgot my charger. Did Jacob give you the message?"

She took a sip of her iced tea, then rested the cup on the railing. "Jacob? No, Kaitlyn sent me a note this morning—"

"Not until this morning?" Lucas frowned. "I called last night around seven."

"We all met up for Mexican food. He was probably stuffing his face with chips." She laughed. "The important thing is that you're here now. So does your grandma really tease you about running from relationships?"

"Yes, she has in the past, but it's not true, and that's definitely not what happened yesterday." He set his cup down and inched closer.

"I had my doubts last night, but I believe you now." She sent him a coy smile.

He reached for her hand. It was soft and warm. "Would you also believe that what started out as a pretend relationship doesn't feel imaginary to me anymore? Megan, I've fallen in love with you and I hope you feel the same. Please, say you'll be my girl—for real this time."

She wrapped her arms around his waist. "Yes. Most definitely yes!"

He took her face between his palms and gently placed his lips on hers. She pulled him close and deepened the kiss.

When they separated, her gaze lifted. "It's true. You *can* hurry love."

He ran his fingers down her cheek. "When it's right, anything is possible." He leaned down for another kiss.

"Glory be!" Grandma Ruby shouted from the promenade. "This is the best birthday ever."

The End

92

# ABOUT THE AUTHOR

Sherry Kyle is an award-winning author and a graduate of Biola University. Her writing credits include five novels and three novellas described as "full of unforgettable characters, quaint settings, and sweet romance," as well as books for children.

Sherry has four children, three biological and one by adoption. When she isn't writing, she enjoys reading, decorating her beach home, taking long walks along the ocean, and watching movies with her husband, Douglas. Sherry and her family live by the coast in Central California. You can sign up for her newsletter and connect with her on her website at www.sherrykyle.com

# PRAISE FOR

# SWEET CRANBERRIES

"Ah, friendship, love, humor and charm all wrapped up in this delightful story about two people whose friendship grows into love during autumn in Nantucket. It grabbed my heart. These two were made for each other and I enjoyed watching them find one another. Highly recommended." ~ 5 stars, Karen O'Connor, author, speaker, writing mentor

"The story comes with some unique surprises I didn't see coming and had a great ending that left me smiling. You just have to read this one. It will make you smile, laugh, and feel compassion for the characters within the pages. Highly recommended." ~ 5 stars, J.E. Grace, Amazon reviewer

"Found this book at the recommendation of a friend. Delightful and sweet tale filled with wonderful small town characters! Lovely, short, read for an autumn weekend!" ~4 stars, CarolynK, Amazon reviewer

"Set in autumn amid the charm of Nantucket, Sweet Cranberries is a delightful novella about giving people a chance and about fresh starts. Sherry Kyle's fun banter and eccentric locals make this a story full of laughter and heart. Enjoy!"
~5 stars, Sarah Sundin, author of historical romance

# CHAPTER ONE

Amanda Richards poured herself a third glass of pink punch and sat in a dining chair on the far side of her parents' family room. With each gift her cousin Emma opened, her friends and family members oohed and aahed and giggled. Emma was the picture of the perfect bride-to-be.

Amanda took another sip of her punch as Emma reached for another package. A nervous flutter danced in Amanda's stomach when Emma untied the pink ribbon. Would she like her gift, or was it more to Amanda's liking?

"Amanda, why are you hiding in the corner?" Her mother's voice pulled at her. "You should join the other women. Maybe they can give you ideas on how to find a date. I hear most women are meeting men online these days. It worked for Emma—"

"You're right, Mom. I'll move closer." She stood and inched her way toward her cousin, stopping her mother from furthering this perpetual conversation, and to see whether Emma liked her gift.

Emma tore the metallic gold wrapping away from the box containing a KitchenAid mixer in matte dried rose.

"It's pink!" Emma grinned. "Won't it look pretty sitting on my kitchen counter? Thank you, Amanda."

She smiled back. "I hope Brandon is okay with the color—"

"He said I could decorate any way I want." Emma moved the heavy mixer to the artisan rug and reached for another present.

"That's Brandon. Isn't my brother the best?" Tiffany piped in.

"That's the sign of a good man right there. Wish we could all find one like him." Melissa, Emma's maid of honor, wrote something down on her clipboard. Was she writing Brandon's qualities or keeping track of the gifts? Amanda pressed her lips to stifle a giggle.

"Let me know if you want me to show you how to use it," Amanda said. After all, what good was a mixer if Emma only wanted to look at it?

When all the presents had been opened, the women moved to form a line at the buffet table. There were several appetizers and finger sandwiches to choose from. On the far end of the table sat pink lemonade cheesecake parfaits served in clear goblets. Emma's maid of honor had gone all out.

"Just think," Mom said, sidling up beside her. "When you're engaged, your maid of honor will give you a bridal shower too. Won't that be fun?"

"Mom, it's not going to happen for a long time." She wanted to say more, but held back. Ever since Amanda's thirtieth birthday a few months ago, her mother had been hounding her to find a man. You'd think it was Mom's biological clock ticking.

Amanda grabbed a gold-colored plate and began filling it.

"Getting married is something most women look forward to, not avoid altogether," Mom said, her voice low.

"Mom! Please. Today is about Emma. Leave me out of it." She hadn't meant to raise her voice.

She looked around the room to see concern etched on everyone's faces. Emma's most of all.

Amanda's cheeks heated. Time to save face and shift the focus. "Melissa, you've outdone yourself. The food and decorations are beautiful!"

She had to get out of there. Could she feign illness? A headache, perhaps? Anything to get away from men-crazy women and her mother's relentless prying and pushing for her to be the next Richards bride.

It wasn't as if she had a hard time finding a date or *wanted* to be single. She'd had her share of boyfriends, but couldn't see herself married to any of them. What was wrong with her? If only she had bigger plans, a new aspiration, or a huge goal to fill her schedule, then maybe Mom would leave her alone.

Working at the bank in the 'insufficient funds' department for the last three years didn't give the impression that she was moving up the corporate ladder. At her last review her boss had said as much. "Amanda, you do a good job, but you're like a square peg in a round hole. A cubicle job might not be the best fit for you. Are you sure you're not meant to be around people instead of numbers?"

Mr. Johnson's words had haunted her all week. Truthfully, she couldn't agree more. But what did that look like? She made decent money, although if she were honest with herself, working at the bank didn't make her happy.

She placed a cucumber sandwich on her plate next to the bruschetta and caprese bite, then picked up a dessert goblet and silverware and moved into the large family room to sit down.

"Amanda, sit here." Emma patted the seat beside her. She obliged.

"What happened back there?" Emma asked. "It isn't like you to hide out in the corner or raise your voice to your mom. You two are close."

"Not lately." She forked a caprese bite. "Mom is pushing too hard. I'm sure it's difficult for her to have a thirty-year-old daughter with no man on the horizon ... because if there is no man, there are no grandbabies." She was going down a rabbit hole Emma didn't need to hear. "Please, forgive me. Like I said, this party isn't about me—it's about you."

"I'm sorry if my bridal shower is making things more difficult for you and your mom." Emma, though high maintenance in many ways, was as sweet as they came.

"Your bridal shower is perfect. Let's enjoy this amazing food!" Amanda popped a nacho chip with dip into her mouth.

Emma laughed. "It is good, isn't it?"

She nodded and hummed a response.

A small lump formed in her throat. Her relationship with Emma would be different when her cousin married Brandon. Amanda wouldn't feel as free to call her to go shopping after work or to the farmer's market on Saturday mornings. Never mind the impromptu hot chocolate nights where they'd sit and talk for hours. It had already been different since Emma started dating Brandon. Now that they were engaged, time with her cousin was in short supply. As happy as she was for Emma, Amanda had to accept the fact she was losing her best friend.

"Say cheese on the count of three. One ... two ... " Her mother snapped a bunch of pictures, most of them with silly poses and goofy grins.

A phone rang in someone's purse. The women scrambled to see whose it was.

Amanda snatched her ringing phone and took off in the direction of the back porch. She slid the glass door shut and answered. "Aunt Linda! We miss you! I wish you could have been here. Emma loved your gift—"

"Is the bridal shower over yet? I couldn't wait a moment longer."

"We're winding down. What's up?"

"Do you have a minute or would you rather I call back later?" Her aunt's voice gave away which one she preferred.

Personally, it felt good to stand outside, breathe the fresh air, and watch the breeze rustle the leaves on the trees. "Now is fine."

"Great. I thought if your mother was still there, you could get her opinion after we're through. I know how close the two of you are."

First Emma and now her aunt. Did everyone in her family feel that way? If only that statement were true these last few months, but Amanda wouldn't correct her. "Go on."

"As your parents might have mentioned, Uncle Greg and I bought an RV. It has been a dream of ours to tour the United States, and now is the time to do it before our knees give way and we're not able to hike and bike, and do all the things we want to do.

"Sounds fun," Amanda said. "But what about your restaurant?"

"Last night, we decided it was time to sell."

Amanda's heart sank. "You're going to sell the Blue Crab Café?" Memories of her childhood flashed through her mind. Trips to Nantucket were the highlight of her summers, and working in the café during her teenaged years had drawn her close to her aunt and uncle. "But you love that place. *I* love that place—"

"That's what I wanted to hear." Aunt Linda's voice rose a notch. "Your uncle and I want to sell the restaurant to you. We want you to become the new owner."

Had she heard correctly?

When she hesitated, her aunt continued. "Since Uncle Greg and I never had children, we want someone in the family to carry on our legacy."

She had to say something. But what, she didn't know. She bit her lower lip, as words started forming in her mind. "I'm honored. And humbled you think I could run The Blue Crab by myself…"

"You won't need to start from scratch. Most of the staff will stay, including our main cook and most of the servers—to make things easier for you."

Amanda kicked at a leaf that had blown onto the back porch. Was this the dream she was looking for? Truth be told, if there were anywhere she'd move to from Boston it would be Nantucket. She enjoyed the small-town life the island offered. And the people were some of the nicest she'd ever met.

"Can you give me a couple of days to think about it?" Amanda asked.

"I know this news must be a bit of a shock. Like I said, talk with your mom. She's your biggest supporter. I'm sure she'll help you make the best decision. And, Amanda, no matter what, Uncle Greg and I love you and want what's best—for you and for us. Keep us posted, okay? And tell everyone hello for me."

Amanda hung up and sat on the back porch swing. Aunt Linda wanted her to be the new owner of the Blue Crab Café. It seemed unimaginable to leave Boston. But instead of wanting to say no and resist, the longer she sat here, the more the idea appealed to her. Her boss's words came to the forefront of her mind again. Even Mr. Johnson could see that she needed a change.

But to run a restaurant? She'd never considered that idea until now.

Her mother poked her head out the sliding glass door. "Amanda, there you are. The guests are leaving. Can you help Melissa and me clean up? We're going to save the decorations. You never know when there'll be another bridal shower in the family..."

Suddenly, the answer to Aunt Linda's question became very clear.

She was moving to Nantucket.

# OTHER NOVELS BY SHERRY KYLE

*Delivered with Love*
*The Heart Stone*
*Watercolor Dreams*
*Road to Harmony*
*Capture Me*
*Forever Yours This Christmas* (novella)
*Sweet Cranberries* (novella)